DARN KNIT ALL

ALL ACCESS SERIES
BOOK 3

EVIE MITCHELL

THUNDER THIGHS PUBLISHING

Paperback ISBN: 978-1-922561-30-5
Audiobook ISBN: 978-1-922561-55-8

Cover designs by Eileen Widjaja and Laras Putri
Editing by Emerald Edits, Aquila Editing and Evermore Editing.
Expert edits by Salt and Sage Books.
Special thanks to Meena, Kevin, Izumi, and the expert readers who wish to remain anonymous for their support.

ACKNOWLEDGEMENT OF COUNTRY

I acknowledge the Traditional Custodians of the lands on which I write, the Ngunnawal people, and pay my respect to elders both past and present.

I acknowledge the continued and deep spiritual relationship of the Australian Aboriginal and Torres Strait Islander peoples to this land, and their unique cultural and spiritual relationships to the land, waters and seas and their rich contribution to society.

DEDICATION

*Dedicated to the worrier warriors, to those who overthink,
overanalyze, and over-caffeinate.
Feel the fear and do it anyway, it's worth it.
I promise.*

*And to my partner-in-crime: You're the cheese to my
existential dread – sharp, comforting, and undeniably
delicious.
Thank you for being my original friends-to-lovers romance.*

Theo

You might be asking yourself how a guy like me ended up on a fashion reality TV show. You may also be asking why I agreed to be a designer's apprentice with no discernible sewing skills.

Cake.

Delicious, fluffy, flour-laden, sugary cake—the beginning of my downfall.

If it weren't for that cake, I'd have never bribed Mai Sakamoto for more. We'd have never developed a friendship. I wouldn't know of her dreams to become a fashion designer. And I sure as hell would never have ended up on a reality TV show to help her chase those dreams.

Real knight in shining armor moves, right?

Our friendship was a match made in heaven... before the show put us up in a one-bed hotel room.

Now my lines are blurry, and I can't help but wonder, could Mai be my perfect fit?

Mai

Every day I'm battling imposter syndrome, anxiety, and abject terror—and why?

Is it for the prize money? Fame? The opportunity for my designs to be seen around the world?

Nope.

It's because of Theo. Beautiful, hilarious, frustrating Theo.

Theodore Garrett believes in me. He believes I've got what it takes to win this crazy competition. He quiets the doubts in my mind, pushing me toward my dream life.

Only, I don't know how to tell him that my dreams don't include fashion shows and exclusive lines, and instead feature... him.

Darn Knit All.

CHAPTER 1
MAI

THEO

Hey, it's Theo Garrett. I got your number from Ren. We need to talk ASAP!!

MAI

Missed call from Mai

Missed call from Mai

Missed call from Mai

PICK UP YOUR PHONE!!! Is Ren okay!?!? CALL ME!!!

THEO

Shit, sorry!! He's fine, I swear! It's just... you made Frankie and Jay's wedding cake, right?

MAI

Wait. This isn't an emergency?!?

THEO

Well, not one involving Ren.

MAI

Okay. Crap. Did you get food poisoning?

THEO

No. Are you crazy? That cake was the bomb diggity. I just can't get the taste out of my mouth. You don't happen to make them regularly, do you?

MAI

Firstly, bomb diggity? Who still uses that? Secondly, wedding cakes? No. That was a one-off.

THEO

I still use it. Bomb diggity is fun to say. But back to the actual question—how about regular cakes?

MAI

Not really...

THEO

Not even if I begged? Or paid?

MAI

Are you really trying to puppy eye me via text?

THEO

Unashamedly yes.

MAI

This is the weirdest conversation...

THEO

I can pay you in cash, services, or goods. Do you have paper needs? If you don't know, I part-own a paper mill with your bestie and my bro. I'm sure we can work something out.

MAI

I'm aware. And, no. I'm good.

THEO

Come on, I'm desperate here. There has to be something you need. I'm tight with Ren, hit me with your requests. Stink bombing his car? Itching powder in his jocks? I'm not above hiding shrimp in his curtain rails.

MAI

Actually, if you find out what he wants for his birthday then I *might* consider making you a cake.

THEO

Hallelujah! I'm on it!

THEO

He wants tickets to the Wild Ones tour.

MAI

You got that in 5 minutes?

THEO

I told you, I was on it. Now, about that cake?

MAI

One layer and I refuse to do fondant.

THEO

Fondant? Bah! That's the devil's food clothing. It's buttercream or ganache all the way!

MAI

I feel like I'm going to regret this.

THEO

What are you talking about? This is the start of a beautiful friendship.

———

THEO

What are your adjectives?

MAI

?? Do you mean my pronouns?

THEO

No, your adjectives

MAI

...? I have no idea. What are yours?

THEO

Hilarious, loyal, and dashingly chaotic

MAI

Holy!!!

MAI

And suddenly everything makes sense
once more

———

MAI

Check this out

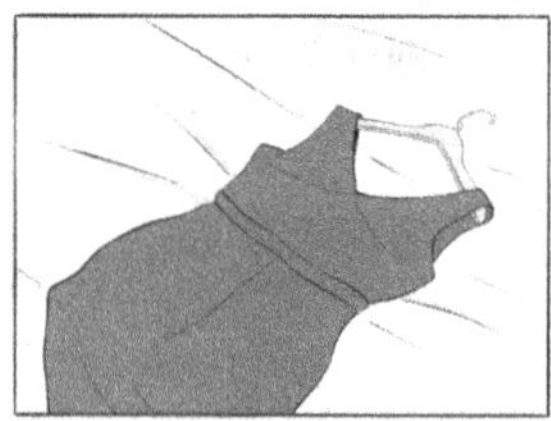

THEO

Holy shit! Now THAT is a dress even I
would wear

MAI

I'd like to see you try

THEO

You know, every time you send me one of these magnificent creations, I get a little FOMO that I can't create something that incredible

MAI

We can't all be filled with awesome

THEO

Alas, this is true

MAI

I could help you, if you wanted? Teach you a few of the basics?

THEO

FUCK YES! I shall be your Padawan— fighting evil one stitch at a time!

MAI

Don't make me regret this

———

THEO

Have you ever looked at something so precious you're worried you'll eat it?

MAI

I take it you're babysitting again?

THEO

Lincoln and Annie are out at some couples' night thing

MAI

Translation: Linc has booked them into a
hotel because Annie needs sleep

THEO

Pretty much. Though why anyone would
want a night away from these kids is
beyond me. Look at them!

MAI

Nawwww. Now I want cuddles

THEO

Come over. All the cuddles from the three
of us you can handle

MAI

Three of you?

THEO

What? You don't platonically cuddle?

MAI

I retract my question

THEO

Should I put the kettle on? Maybe order
some pizza?

MAI

I shouldn't

THEO

Shouldn't you?

MAI

I'll be over soon

———

MAI

Q?

THEO

Shoot

MAI

Do you believe in love at first sight?

THEO

Absolutely

MAI

Wait. Really?

THEO

Have you seen my niece and nephew??? First time I saw them I knew I would do anything for them. ANYTHING! They're kidnapped and sold into the human trafficking trade while on a European vacation? You better believe I'm calling Liam Neeson for pointers

MAI

But what about romantic love? Do you ever think people look at each other and just… know?

THEO

Depends

MAI

On?

THEO

Are they holding a triple layer buttercream peanut butter chocolate cake?

MAI

Be serious!

THEO

No. Not unless they're fated to be together or some weird past life soul mates (*cough* Linc and Annie *cough*). Those are the lucky ones. The rest of us poor souls have to make do with sampling the buffet until we find our match

MAI

Theodore! Be still my heart! I never took you for a romantic!

THEO

I'm like a good meringue—crispy on the outside, marshmallow on the inside

MAI

And far too pretentious for your own good

———

THEO

I've been thinking about your question from last week

MAI

Which one?

THEO

The love at first sight

MAI

Mm?

THEO

Do YOU believe in it?

MAI

Not for me. Other people maybe, but
not me

THEO

Why not you?

MAI

I'm demisexual

THEO

You only love GODS?!?

MAI

That's correct. Out of all the possible
people in the world, I chose to love a God.
Hades, to be precise.

MAI

How did you even get to that idea?

THEO

Andddddddd I just Googled. Ignore me and
my ignorance. My mind jumped to
demigods for some reason. Let's blame
Loki's chaotic bi energy

MAI

You're forgiven now that you're putting in
the work. But do you get why love at first
sight isn't exactly something I understand?

THEO

I'm beginning to. What prompted the
question?

MAI

Romance novel. I loved it but it felt unrealistic. Who just falls in love at a glance? How do you know they're not a terrible person and you don't just want their body?

THEO

The world works in mysterious ways. I wouldn't put past life soul mates out of your mind just yet

MAI

I appreciate your indulgence on this topic

THEO

You are welcome, friend

———

THEO

Can I ask a personal question?

MAI

You can. Doesn't mean I'll answer it

THEO

Fair. How does the dating thing work when you're demisexual?

MAI

Slowly. Painfully so. It's mostly me waking up one day realizing I have a crush on a friend or a colleague and suddenly feeling awkward about it

THEO

Ah. I see. Well, if it makes you feel any better, my regular dating life is less slow burn and more glacial iceberg

MAI

LOL. I take it the date didn't go well?

THEO

Let's just say she wasn't exactly impressed with my Kermit the Frog impression. I did win the trivia night though

MAI

Never change, Theo. Never, ever change

———

MAI

After our talk last night, I realized I didn't explain what my demisexuality looks like

THEO

Go on

MAI

It's not like I don't get sexual feelings. I do. I often feel sexually attracted to people, but to do so I need an emotional connection. Sometimes I have that emotional connection, but my body isn't interested. Other times I have that emotional connection and it's like my body is revved up to ten thousand on the horny scale

THEO

It's subjective

MAI

Yes! And there's nothing I can do to control it. It's kind of an either/or

THEO

Does that mean you don't ever… jiggle the monkey?

MAI

...?

THEO

You know, flick the bean?

MAI

You mean masturbate.

THEO

If you must be crude, yes

MAI

😊 You're so mature... but the answer
is yes

THEO

Girl, same

MAI

I assumed that might be the case...

———

MAI

I had a panic attack today

THEO

Damn What do you need? How can I help?

MAI

Nothing. I just

THEO

Just?

THEO

Mai, you there?

MAI

Sorry, I didn't mean to send that

THEO

Talk to me. Or don't, whatever you need to
do. Just know I'm here

MAI

Sorry for bothering you

THEO

You're the furthest thing from a bother. You
wanna talk?

MAI

No. But thank you

THEO

Any time. Seriously

MAI

Did you send me a stress ball in the shape
of Ren's head?

THEO

I can neither confirm nor deny

MAI

Well, if it was you, thank you. It made me
laugh!

———

THEO

What do you think?

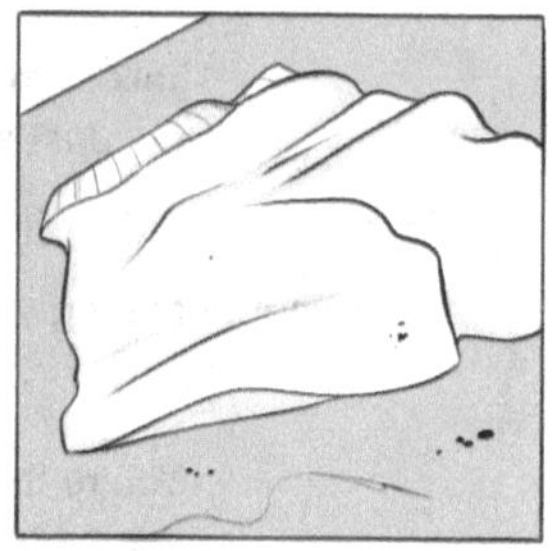

MAI

WTF is that?

THEO

My first sewing attempt, can't you tell?

MAI

Theo. Is that BLOOD???

THEO

Only a little. Do you like it?

MAI

It's a great shirt!

THEO

They're shorts...

MAI

Shorts! Damn autocorrect...

THEO

Somehow I don't believe you

———

MAI

I can't breathe

THEO

Gif of breathing timer

MAI

Thank you. Damn

THEO

What happened?

MAI

I had a dress fitting with a bride, and her mother started freaking out about sizing because the bride put on a little weight. It's not a big deal but the mother lost it and started screaming

THEO

I will never understand the pressure weddings put on people. You okay now?

MAI

No. But I will be

THEO

Chicken wings?

MAI

Not sure I'll be very good company

THEO

You're always great company. Come on, you know you want some finger licking meaty goodness

MAI

Thanks for tonight <3

THEO

Any time. Though next time I'm ordering extra fries

MAI

You say that every time

THEO

And every time I mean it

————

THEO

How do you feel about G-strings?

MAI

For me or for you?

THEO

Good question. Both?

MAI

In what context are we talking?

THEO

There needs to be a context?

MAI

Oh, so you've never actually worn a G-string

THEO

How can you tell?

MAI

Theo, one does not wear one for no reason. The pain, the discomfort, the picking it out of your ass. There are only three reasons to subject yourself to such an event,

1. No panty lines for tight clothing

2. You want to get lucky

3. Laundry day and it's all that is left

Which is it?

THEO

Linc's bachelor party. We want to buy one for the groom

MAI

Of course you create a 4th reason

———

THEO

You ever feel like you're destined to be alone?

MAI

I take it the date isn't going well?

THEO

Understatement. She stood me up

MAI

Ouch

THEO

My only consolation is the bar felt so bad they shouted me free fries

MAI

Mmmmmm fries

THEO

Wanna come share them with me? You're only around the corner…

MAI

Will there be chicken wings?

THEO

I can make some appear

MAI

See you in 5

. . .

I strode into the bar, my gaze scanning the room for a familiar dark-brown head and spotted Theo waving frantically from his seat at the bar. I lifted my chin in acknowledgement, rolling my eyes and grinning at his exuberance as I began to make my way through the tables to him.

If anyone had asked me how to describe Theo, I'd have been at a loss. Sure, I could describe the way his dark hair flopped over his green eyes, or the fact he often made me feel small and protected thanks to his height and muscular build. I could comment on how he always wore plaid and jeans, with the right leg of his pants cut off at the knee for easy access to his prosthetic. I could describe how he— unlike his twin—was always ready with a smile, laughing his way through life.

But all of that was superficial. The beauty of Theo wasn't in his looks; his beauty came from the way he made you feel. He reminded me of a hug, or the first sunny day after a bitter winter—sweet and desperately needed.

Theo had to be the very definition of a golden-retriever-type personality. Hyperactive, adorably awkward, passionately protective, lovingly loyal and hilariously friendly. When you became one of his people, he did whatever he could to make you happy.

Which is why I'd changed out of PJs and pulled on a bra to haul myself down to the local bar on a Wednesday night to comfort him.

These were sacrifices I made for friends.

"What happened this time?" I asked, sliding into the seat beside his.

He held up his phone for me to see. "Ghosted. She texted right up until fifteen minutes after the date had been due to start then said, 'can't come' and blocked me on the app."

"Rude." I leaned over to swipe a fry from the basket in front of him. "Your bad luck with potential partners is becoming legendary."

Theo slumped on the barstool. "Tell me about it. At this rate I'm going to end up dying alone."

I raised my hand, flagging down the bartender. "At least you're trying. My dating life is dryer than the Sahara Desert."

"She arrived," the cute bartender said, grinning at Theo.

"No, this is my friend, Mai. Mai meet Aiden. He's been keeping me company for the last two hours."

Aiden reached across the bar to shake my hand. "Pleasure."

I eyed him, sizing him up as a potential date for Theo. "Lovely to meet you, Aiden. Do you happen to be single?" I jerked my thumb at Theo. "'Cause this big guy is looking."

He chuckled. "Alas no. I also happen to be about to leave the Cove. But if all of that ever falls apart—" He winked at Theo. "—I'll give you a call."

"See?" Theo said with a dramatic sigh. "I'm cursed."

"You're not cursed." I tilted my head to one side as I considered the selection of non-alcoholic beverages available to me. "Apple cider, please."

"Good choice." Aiden pulled a bottle free, cracking

open the lid. "This one's local. It's from Red Dog Brewery, and the apples are grown at the 4H Farm."

I sipped, enjoying the tart sweetness. "Oh, it's good."

Aiden grinned. "Call when you want a refill."

He left us to serve another customer.

Theo reached for a chicken wing. "Sorry for dragging you out here."

I shrugged. "I was watching reruns of *Astipia's Next Top Model*. I think you've saved me from myself."

Red flags began to wave when he didn't even smile.

"Hey." I touched a hand to his leg. "You okay?"

"Sorry, just in a shitty mood."

"Because whoever she is stood you up?"

He nodded then shook his head then huffed. "I don't know. It's just... never mind."

"You wanna talk about it?"

"No." He hesitated. "Maybe? No. Definitely not."

He dropped the uneaten chicken wing on his napkin. Warning bells began to wail, for Theo was a man who devoured everything within sight. For him not to be eating? The situation had to be serious.

"Come on," I coaxed. "I'll be your sounding board."

For the umpteenth time since I'd sat down, Theo huffed and sighed and huffed again.

"I'm just being ungrateful." He ran a hand through his hair. "I need to get over myself."

I waved a dismissive hand. "Stop putting yourself down. Let it out."

"I've got a good home. A good job. A great family." He stopped, making a frustrated noise.

"But?" I prompted when he didn't continue.

"But. That's a good question. I should be grateful but... Linc and Annie are the brains behind the business, I'm just the supervisor helping them toward their vision. I live in a rental. My family is primarily their family. I don't know, sometimes I just feel...." He shrugged.

"Like you're a third wheel in your own life?"

"Oof! Right in the feels there, Mai." He rubbed his chest.

"You know, you're not the only one who feels like that sometimes." I tossed a fry in my mouth, chewing thoughtfully. "Or maybe more than sometimes."

"Try all the time."

I frowned. "That doesn't seem healthy."

"I know." He shuffled on his seat, one hand dropping to absently rub at the liner covering his right knee. I knew some of his story. He'd been in a car crash over a decade ago that had pinned him in the vehicle. They'd had to perform a transtibial amputation—removing his leg from below the knee—in order to free him.

I'd known of Theo before the accident but only in the way I knew of most people in this small town. We hadn't been friends or even closely acquainted. At some point over the last decade, he and my brother, Ren, had become friends, and through Ren I'd begun to know Theo. But it hadn't been until the last few years that we'd gotten close.

"I guess the question becomes, what are you going to do about it?" I asked, slicking another fry through some ketchup.

"I don't know. How do you deal with it?"

I chuckled. "I don't. I just avoid thinking too hard about the details."

A drop of sauce slipped from my fry on the journey to my mouth, splattering on my jean leg.

"Damn." I slid from the stool, grabbing some napkins. "I'll be right back. Let me clean this off before it stains."

I washed the stain in the bathroom and returned to find Theo bent over his phone.

I slid back onto the stool beside him. "Miss me?"

His head jerked up, his eyes dancing. "I've figured it out."

I arched one eyebrow.

"How we're gonna start living! No more third wheel in our own lives. To kick us off, I'm sending in your application for this." He handed me his phone.

I glanced down to find it opened to a website—*PerfectFitContest.com.*

"What is this?"

"It's a fashion competition." He bounced in his chair. "They're searching for up-and-coming designers to profile on their reality TV show. The prize is your own show and a shit-ton of money."

I scrolled through the page, shaking my head. "I can't. I'm not good enough for something like this."

"Psh." Theo plucked the phone out of my hand. "I'm entering you."

"Theo!"

"Too late," he said, his thumbs flying over the screen. "This is your challenge."

"I'll never get in."

"Then there's nothing to lose."

I couldn't argue with his logic.

He glanced up, seeing my expression. "You're an incredible designer, Mai. You deserve to at least try."

He held the phone out to me. "Yes or no?"

The submit button stared out at me from the screen, taunting me.

"Fuck it." I hit it then shoved his hand away. "Now drop it before I start overthinking this."

He chuckled. "You're going to overthink it anyway."

I poked my tongue out at him, then waggled a finger in his direction. "What about you? You've thrown me under a bus, how are you going to challenge yourself?"

He chuckled, spreading his arms wide. "I'll leave that in your capable hands. If we can't kick-start our own lives, why not kick-start each other's?"

"You like to live dangerously."

He grinned, ruffling my hair. "Bring it on."

CHAPTER 2

MAI

No one talks about how much work it is living with anxiety. Oh, sure. They'll tell you how tiring and emotionally draining it feels to operate in a constant state of heightened emotions. But no one talks about being up until 3am the night before a big meeting to research five different routes in case the one you take is congested or closed for repairs.

Plan B? More like plans A through triple Z.

You know who needs to be running emergency service departments? Anyone with high anxiety. We plan for all contingencies.

I looked down at the cell phone clutched in my clammy hand, trying to breathe through the near-overwhelming panic that clawed up my throat and constricted my chest.

> *Dear Ms. Sakamoto,*
>
> *We are pleased to invite you to participate in Perfect Fit, a reality fashion design competition series hosted by Michelle Conliam.*
>
> *You'll be challenged to design cutting-edge creations which will be judged by our panel of expert designers, Minerva Devillian, Alison Louis, and Erike Baretti.*

The email continued but I couldn't, my anxiety hitting a level of fear I hadn't experienced in years.

Huddled on the dressing room floor of Bloom Boutique, I faced myself in not one, not two, but three mirrors—each reflecting a woman on the edge of a breakdown.

My black hair fell from my ponytail to frame my face in a frizzy mess of strands. My cheeks were flushed, and my dark eyes were wide, the pupils dilated. My skin had turned a clammy, mottled color, while cold sweat dotted my brow. My chest rose and fell with quick, short breaths as I struggled to regain control.

I'd never had a breakdown in front of a mirror before, and a part of me—that wasn't freaking the fuck out—found the entire experience endlessly fascinating.

I'm going to strangle Theo.

My stomach clutched and clawed as I forced myself to slow my breathing.

I am safe. I am in a safe space.

My therapist's words whispered through my ears, her voice gentle and encouraging.

Ground yourself, feet flat on the ground, hands on your legs or the floor.

Through sheer force of will I moved into a sitting position. With my back resting against the cool wall of the stall, I raised my knees to plant my feet and pressed my palms to the carpeted floor.

Take a breath, hold for a beat then recite three things you can see.

I sucked in a gulp, holding the air in my pounding chest, doing as she'd taught me.

Normally, I could hold off the worst of it, putting on a brave face and batting away any suggestion of concern with a smile. I knew how to mask my anxiety behind over-performance and apologies, hiding my fears behind a laughing façade until I could crumble alone.

Today, those masks had failed, allowing a torrid flood of emotions to crush me.

"White walls, silver mirrors, a pink chair."

I sucked in another breath, forcing myself to continue to name what I could see in the room.

"A glittering chandelier, a white door, a silver clothes rack."

A tentative knock on the dressing room door interrupted my recitation.

"Mai? You okay in there?" Bloom's co-owner and my boss, Yasmin Prince, tapped on the door again. "Can I come in?"

I sucked in big gulps of air, desperately wishing I could deny her.

"Sure," I forced myself to answer.

She pushed the door open slightly, spying me sitting on the floor.

"Oh, Mai."

She hurried in, her pregnant belly preceding her.

"Let me—" She made a move to crouch.

"Stop!" I held out a hand pointing at the chair in the corner of the bridal change room.

"Good idea." She took the seat with a groan, her expression grudging. "I thought I'd be a beautiful pregnant unicorn, one of those women who glow and waddle but in a cute and attractive kind of way." She sighed, leaning back with another groan. "Instead, I'm battling stretch marks and back pain, not to mention the pregnancy acne, and I waddle like a disgruntled duck."

She lied, of course. Pregnant with her first child, Yasmin glowed with the kind of joy that only true love could bring.

She bore an uncanny resemblance to a fairy-tale princess with her ebony hair, rich tan skin, and warm mahogany eyes. She radiated peace and calm—it was one of the reasons I'd wanted to work at Bloom Boutique.

That she happened to be an incredible seamstress and generous teacher were icing on an already delicious cake.

"Ducks are cute," I managed to mutter, grateful she hadn't asked me how I felt. I wasn't sure I'd be able to temper my response.

"Sure, the fluffy babies. Not the horrific older ones. You know they're super violent? Caleb and I watched a documentary on it." She placed a hand over her stomach. "I don't think I've cried that much since I watched *The NeverEnding Story*. It felt like my childhood was being shattered."

I forced a smile.

"And don't tell me it's pregnancy hormones." She waggled a finger at me. "I might be seven months and impacted by every other side effect known to woman, but not that one."

Maeve Oakley, Bloom's other co-owner, poked her head in, her grin wide on her pixie-like face. "Are we doing an impromptu staff meeting? Should I bring alcohol-free wine?"

"Grape juice." Yasmin rolled her eyes. "God forbid. I don't think I can stomach any more of that shit. My mother-in-law thinks it's a great option at family dinners."

My racing heart began to slow, the rigidity in my muscles easing as they bickered back and forth, ignoring me. Their familiar banter and the comfort of their presence helped ground me.

"Better?" Yasmin asked when I shifted into a cross-legged position.

"Yeah. Sorry."

She waved me off. "You wanna talk about it?"

The phone sat in my lap, taunting me.

"I...." My throat closed, panic rising once more.

"Hey!"

I snapped my head up to find Maeve glaring at me.

"I'm"—she stabbed two fingers at herself then at me—"talking to that devil on your shoulder right now. Our Mai is awesome. She's amazing. She doesn't have time for doubting herself. Spill your worries before the devil eats away at you."

"I...." I couldn't speak life into this moment.

Beyond grateful for these two amazing women, I fought to get a handle on the anxiety beast that rode my back and gnawed in my chest.

Shoving the phone in Maeve's direction, I closed my eyes, repeating her words.

I'm amazing. I'm awesome. I don't have time to doubt myself.

Maeve took the phone, and I listened as she read it aloud to Yasmin, both of them squealing with excitement.

"Oh my God, Mai! This is incredible." Yasmin clapped her hands together. "What an opportunity. I didn't even know you applied."

My stomach dipped, my mind disconnecting from my body. "I didn't. Theo nominated me."

"Who cares who did what—the important thing is you're *in*." Maeve shook the phone at me. "If you don't say yes to this, I *will* disown you. Erike Baretti will see your designs. Erike-freaking-Baretti!"

I couldn't help but note a tiny part of me, buried deep under the panic, thrilled alongside her. Michelle Conliam, Minerva Devillian, Alison Louis, and Erike Baretti were legends in the fashion world, and to work on something they might see would be a once-in-a-lifetime opportunity.

Holy shit. They might see my designs.

The little spark of excitement died under the weight of my anxiety, smothered by my fear of being seen. The idea of being judged, of having my designs laid bare terrified me. I'd rather walk down Main Street naked than be that vulnerable.

I swallowed, trying to draw moisture into the desert of my mouth. "I'm going to say no."

They froze.

"What?" Yasmin reached out to place a hand on my knee. "Why?"

I gestured at her stomach. "I can't leave the store."

"Of course you fucking can," she snapped. "Maeve is more than capable of running this place."

Maeve nodded vigorously.

"It's coming into wedding season," I protested. "I know how busy this time of year gets."

"We'll organize to backfill you." Yasmin waved her hand dismissively. "Right, Maeve?"

Maeve nodded vehemently. "You deserve this. Seriously, Mai, you have to."

"But the baby—"

"We have time to figure everything out before bubba

arrives." Yasmin caught my gaze. "Listen to me. I *refuse* to allow you to squander what is a life-changing opportunity. This has the potential to set you up for life, Mai. You can conquer your dreams. Just think about the prize money, the recognition."

The scrutiny, the self-doubt, the judgment.

My heart kicked into overdrive as sweat trickled down my back.

"What if I'm not good enough?" I whispered, giving voice to my greatest fear. "What if I fail?"

"And what if you succeed?" Maeve countered. She crouched beside me, placing her hand on my opposite knee. "What if you win the whole damn thing?"

"I wouldn't know what to do with the money. All I've ever wanted is to create beautiful pieces of clothing." I gestured at the dressing room. "And we do that every day."

"So you buy into Bloom. Or you set up your own boutique. Or you keep working here part-time and I sell a line of your clothing. Or you do a million other things the prize money and recognition will afford you." Yasmin squeezed my knee. "The choice is yours, my friend."

"Buy into Bloom?" My heart stuttered, a near-overwhelming desire welling up in me.

She leaned back into her chair, groaning with the effort. "If you want. Maeve already did and"—she patted her stomach—"with this one and no doubt more kids on the way, I won't have the time I once did to build the business. We've been talking about bringing on another partner to help out. You're an incredible designer and wonderful colleague—not to mention good friend." She shrugged. "Why not?"

A world of possibility began to open for me.

"Are you sure?" I asked Maeve.

"We already discussed it." She flicked a grin at Yasmin. "We didn't know that you were interested, but I agree with Yasmin. If this store is your dream, then let's do it."

Some people might envision success as sold-out runway shows in Milan or Paris. Some might think of a fashion house in New York or London. My idea of success had always involved Capricorn Cove, the small island town I've called home for most of my life.

I loved everything about our close-knit community, nestled in the heart of the Isle of Astipia. The certainty and comfort of my life here, the changing seasons, the familiar faces—I couldn't imagine ever leaving.

When I pictured my future, I imagined a quiet house in the suburbs with a flower garden and fantastic fire pit. I pictured two-point-five kids and a hamster. I pictured a partner who adored me, and a library and fabric room.

I pictured a quiet, fulfilling life, full of love, laughter, joy, and contentment.

And above all else, certainty.

I raised my head. "I want it. If I win and get the money, I want to buy in."

They grinned.

"And if I don't," I swallowed. "I'll find the money."

Somehow.

My finances weren't exactly in the best shape. The boutique paid well, but our small town had experienced a growth surge in the last few years, bumping up the price of housing. I had a meager savings fund tucked away but that wouldn't get anywhere close to the kind of money I needed to become a partner in Bloom.

Maeve patted my hand. "We'll cross that bridge when we come to it. Now, show me the examples Theo sent in to wow the judges." She made a grabbing motion with her hand.

I flicked through my phone, finding the three designs.

She shuffled closer to Yasmin, tilting the phone her way. Together they ooh-ed and ahh-ed over the designs.

"The drape of the dress," Yasmin raved, shaking her head. "I want it. It'd be perfect for my maternity shoot."

"And the bias cut on this skirt? Inspired," Maeve agreed, flicking between the two. "I love the coat. The shape and colors remind me of a *kimono*."

I hesitated. "It's for my dad. He had an award event at his work."

"It's gorgeous. You should do more pieces that incorporate your heritage into your designs, they're stunning." Maeve handed me back the phone and pushed to a stand, dusting off her legs. "Do you need a hand, momma?" She wiggled her fingers at Yasmin, grinning.

Yasmin's mouth twisted into a disgruntled smile. "If you insist."

With exaggerated grunts and groans, Maeve hauled her out of the chair, both of them pausing in the doorway.

"We love you, babe." Yasmin tapped on the dressing room door. "Whatever you decide."

They left me alone, closing the door behind them.

With a long, slow sigh, I reached for my phone and read the email again, this time with new, hopeful eyes.

I could do this. I could try, and if I won I could—

As I read, my hope skittered off the rails, crashing and burning at the side of the road.

*You and your partner are expected to
arrive no later than 7 September.*

Partner? What partner?

I read back over the email, and sure enough, there it
was. The twist on this year's competition—they wanted
couples to compete together for the prize.

*Let this competition be the start of
your legacy together.*

"Thank God."

With a relieved sigh, I texted a screenshot of the email
to Theo with the couples' clause circled in bright red.

MAI

Next time, we read the fine print

I hit send with a wry chuckle.

"All that stress for nothing. What a waste."

I glanced up, catching my reflection in the mirrors. My
relief was evident, but there was something else there too—a
flicker of disappointment.

Despite the anxiety, doubts, and the little voice in my
head that said I couldn't do this, Yasmin and Maeve had
convinced me I should try.

No. I *wanted* to try.

But my dating life had been as dry as the Sahara for the
last five years. Characters from my favorite novels were as
close as I got to romance these days. And yet, even as I tried
to persuade myself that it was for the best, I couldn't shake
off the competition entirely.

I pressed a hand to the wall of the bridal suite, breathing in the quiet of the room. I could co-own this business. These walls could be my walls. But I needed money to make this dream into reality.

I looked down at my phone, the email still glowing on the screen. The knowledge that they wanted me, had looked at my application and designs and liked what they saw, stirred a strange sense of longing. I didn't need approval from my peers—but goodness if it didn't feel good to know I had it.

Which made me wonder, what if this wasn't the end of the story? What if it was just the beginning of a new chapter, one I hadn't even realized I wanted to write?

I shook my head, laughing at myself.

"Come on," I said, clicking the light off in the dressing room. "Back to work."

CHAPTER 3
THEO

THEO

I need a favor

MAI

Uh-oh

THEO

Why uh-oh? What have I ever done to
deserve this reaction?

MAI

You're really going to ask that question?

THEO

Yes! I deserve an answer!

MAI

Where should I start? How about the
ball game

THEO

You didn't even like those shoes

MAI

True. But I like not walking home in vomit

THEO

One example. Big deal

MAI

And the cow incident

THEO

Could have happened to anyone

MAI

And yet it happened to you... and me. You
know I lost money when I sold that car

THEO

So... is this a no on the favor?

MAI

It depends. Are you expecting any form of
bodily fluid to be involved?

THEO

I'll ask someone else

MAI

Good thinking

A sea breeze ruffled my hair, carrying the salty tang of the sea. Waves crashed rhythmically against the shore, the sound at once familiar and soothing.

In the distance, seagulls called to each other, searching for unattended scraps as young parents played in the sun with their kids, making the most of these last days of warmth before the autumn storms rolled in.

I loved Capricorn Cove, with its wild coastline and

dramatic seasons. As much as small-town life sometimes chafed, I couldn't imagine living anywhere else.

"What's going on between you and my sister?"

I turned away from the view to see Ren stabbing a stray tomato piece with his fork. We'd met for lunch in a local park on one of Ren's rare days off. The guy worked for the local fire department—a department that currently faced a near chronic shortage of staff. If I didn't have an overwhelming fear of heights, I'd be tempted to join just to help remove some of the shadows from under his eyes.

Not that I'd pass the physical. The fire department wasn't exactly looking for a guy with a prosthetic leg.

"What do you mean by 'going on'?" I asked, making quotation marks with my fingers as I shifted on the bench seat of the ancient picnic table.

"You know what I mean." Ren stabbed another tomato. "Are you dating?"

My eyebrows lifted. "Dating?"

Ren's dark eyes met mine. "Stop answering my questions with questions. You heard me. Are you dating?"

One couldn't miss the family resemblance between the siblings. From their dark eyes, button noses, and black hair that held the same adorable cow lick, one glance could tell they were related.

Only, I wasn't attracted to Ren. My attraction to his sister, however... well, she was a whole other story. And one I didn't let myself dwell on for too long.

"Dating," I murmured, tasting the word on my tongue. "Are we dating? I must have missed the memo."

Ren shifted, the muscles in his arms flexing. "Don't give me shit, Theo. I wanna know."

I leaned back, enjoying torturing him far more than I should. "Why do you ask?"

He dropped his fork to list the reasons on his fingers. "You're always at her house. You're regularly seen together eating out. You're happier than you have been in five years. You text her religiously. She constantly talks about you when we hang out. You—"

"Wait. Dial back. She talks about me? What does she say?"

Ren flapped a hand dismissively. "Stop grinning like the cat who ate the cream and answer the question."

I knew Mai wasn't interested in me, but knowing I was on her mind pleased the fuck out of me.

"Have you asked Mai?"

He frowned, glancing away. "She said you're just friends."

I couldn't stop my pleased chuckle. There was something rather satisfying about riling him up.

"There you have it. We're just friends."

"Just friends my ass," Ren muttered darkly, picking up his fork. "You're both too happy to be just friends."

"Ah, and now we get to the real issue." I pretended to hold a notepad and pen, giving Ren my best upper-crust British accent. "And when did your sexual dysfunction start? Was it before or after you met Flo—"

A slice of cucumber hit me square in the forehead.

"You fucker." I caught the piece as it fell, tossing it in my mouth. "Ooh, pickled. Yum."

He shot me the bird. "This isn't about me."

"It absolutely is." I leaned in. "You could just tell her, you know."

For a second, naked longing flashed across Ren's face before he shuttered his emotions.

"We're talking about you and Mai."

I guess we're ignoring his obsession with Flo.

"There's nothing here beyond friendship," I answered easily.

And the occasional wet dream.

I brushed off the errant thought. "Your sister and I have built a friendship based on a mutual love of cake, reality TV, and obscure pop references. And she's trying to teach me how to sew. It's going well."

If we didn't count the trip to the hospital last month. It was fine; the stitches had only left a tiny scar.

Ren did not seem reassured. "Look, I'm not going to warn you off—God knows you'd treat her like a queen."

"Thank you," I drawled dryly. "That means a lot."

"And having you for a brother-in-law would be great."

"Hanging with my buddy every major holiday?" I nodded solemnly. "We'd be living the dream."

"But, and this is a big but."

"You cannot lie?" I asked, cocking an eyebrow.

Ren ignored my joke. "Mai is...."

"Awesome, brilliant, wonderful, intelligent, successful, witty, kind, generous, a wonderful human?" I prompted.

"Conflicted. She deserves so much more than she allows herself to have." Ren held my gaze. "I don't want to see her hurt."

"You think I'd hurt her?" I asked lightly. "I didn't realize I was the devil."

It hurt to know your best friend thought you weren't

good enough for his sister. Sure, it was all hypothetical since Mai and I were just friends. But still, it hurt.

"No." Ren scrubbed a hand over his face. "Shit, I'm fucking this up."

"Yeah, you are." I crossed my arms over my chest, my foot tapping under the table. "Don't mince words trying to search for the right ones. Just spit out the imperfect and we'll work out what you mean."

He grinned, shaking his fork at me. "See? That's what I mean. You'd be easy to fall in love with, Theo. You're far too charming and good-looking for any one woman."

I tilted my head to one side. "You hitting on me, Sakamoto? 'Cause I can safely say, you're not my type."

He snorted. "You wish." He ran a hand over his chest. "This is more than you could ever handle." He sobered. "But seriously, Theo. I know my sister—perhaps better than she knows herself sometimes. Be careful with her. Okay?"

I nodded, hiding my frustration. I understood he was the big brother swooping in to ensure that Mai was looked after—but fuck it. We both deserved better. Mai could look after herself, and he'd known me for long enough to know I'd rather be hit in the face with a baseball bat than hurt her.

We returned to our lunch, chewing quietly as we enjoyed the late summer sun. Autumn would be here soon, and with it the quiet fall of leaves and changing of the seasons. But for now, the park burst with activity as families enjoyed the warm weather.

"Why the interrogation?" I asked, breaking our silence. "It's not like Mai and me are anything new. If you had concerns, why not raise them years ago?"

Ren hesitated. "You've become a big part of her life. Call me a remiss brother for not having spoken to you earlier about taking care with her."

I didn't buy that for a minute. The guy could be called a lot of things, but an absent brother wasn't one of them. I thought about defending myself but shrugged off the impulse. Either he trusted me or he didn't. Nothing I said would change that.

"Was this all you wanted to talk about?" I asked, tilting my head back to catch more rays on my skin. "You could have texted."

"No." Ren began to pack up his lunchbox. "You also owe me a hundred bucks."

"For what?"

He stood, brushing down his jeans. "For losing our bet."

I racked my brains trying to remember what foolish thing I'd agreed to this time.

"Nope, can't remember any bets."

Ren pulled a bedraggled scrap of paper from his jean pocket, tossing it down on the table.

I picked up the worn sheet, unfolding it to find my messy handwriting scrawled across the face.

I, Theodore "Theo" Garrett, owe Ren Sakamoto $100 if I am not married by my thirty-third birthday.

God damn it.

We'd all filled out these stupid slips after Annie and

Linc's wedding. We'd been drunk and high on endorphins. I couldn't remember why we'd done it or what anyone had committed to, but it appeared that Ren hadn't forgotten.

"The fact you've kept this from an event that occurred three years ago is disturbing."

"No, it's a testament to my commitment to winning a bet."

I wadded up the slip and tossed it at him. "Joke's on you, my birthday's not for another two months."

Ren laughed, shoving his containers into his bag. "Brother, with your dating history? I'm a shoo-in for this cash. Short of a quickie wedding to a mail-order bride, I'm about to be a hundred bucks richer."

I threw him a haughty look. "Says the man who hasn't had a date in five years. How's that hand going?"

He swung his backpack over his shoulder. "Pay up, Garrett. I'll take cash, card or goods and services."

I offered him a middle finger instead. "Is this why you dragged me out here? To make sure I didn't get hitched to your sister?"

Ren walked backward, laughing smugly. "As if she'd ever say yes to you."

With that shit-talk, he turned, heading for his motorcycle.

"Just for that, I'm gonna ask her!" I yelled at his retreating back.

He flicked me the bird.

"Wait, what was your bet?"

He twisted, his lips quirking into a smile. "As if I'd ever tell."

Muttering under my breath about annoying friends, I

reached for my phone ready to convince Mai to help me drive her brother crazy when it chirped, the screen lighting with Mai's name.

"Speak of the woman and she shall appear."

MAI

Next time, we read the fine print

I tilted my head to one side, trying to remember what new mess I'd gotten myself into.

THEO

What have I done now? Did I sign a contract that requires llamas? Cause I can get us llamas. I know a guy

Ren's motorcycle roared down the street, the pipes rumbling across the bay.

THEO

By the way, I was just having lunch with Ren. Do you want to get married? It'll drive your brother crazy

MAI

Funny you should say that... read your email

Intrigued, I clicked the link she'd sent me.

Dear Ms. Sakamoto,

We are pleased to invite you to participate in Perfect Fit, a reality fashion design competition series hosted by Michelle Conliam.

THEO

Holy Shit!! IT HAPPENED!! MAI!! YOU'RE GONNA BE FAMOUS!!

MAI

Keep reading

I frowned and clicked back, scanning the contents. It took me three read throughs before I registered the catch.

> *This year, we're profiling design couples. Be it Stella McCartney and Alasdhair Willis, or Rick Owens and Michèle Lamy, these famous couples became better designers because of the love they shared for each other and their fashion. Watching two people push each other to greater heights is an act of love our audience desires to see.*
>
> *Good designers create memorable pieces, great designers build legacies.*

I hit dial, my heart sinking. She picked up on the first ring.

"I'm sorry." I ran a hand through my hair. "We can fix this."

"You signed us up for *Love Island* with sewing machines," Mai said, her tone dryly amused. "Considering I'm as single as a nun, I'm not really sure how we fix it."

"Fuck, Mai. You deserve to have your dreams realized. I'm sorry for being a fuck-up."

"You're not a fuck-up," she said loyally.

I snorted, begging to differ. Lincoln, my twin, had always been the wanted son—I was the unexpected spare. Born a minute too late, some of my earliest memories were of my parents telling me how little they cared for me and my poor decisions.

I pinched the bridge of my nose, sucking in a breath.

I knew better than to be impulsive, and yet with one of the people I cared about most I'd been just that. And worse, it had resulted in her being offered everything she wanted—only to have it snatched from her at the first step.

"At least I don't have to be on national TV. No one wants to see a woman having a nervous breakdown every five minutes." Despite her joking tone, I could hear the undercurrent of her disappointment.

I needed to make this right.

"Maybe it's not as bad as it looks," I said, trying to inject some hope into the situation. "I mean, we could email them and get some clarity as to what they mean by 'couples.' Maybe there's an opportunity to—"

"They mean dating, de facto, or married." She huffed out a little breath. "I already checked the fine print."

I deflated like a lead balloon. "Damn."

"Yeah."

"I'm sorry. You deserve the chance to show the world your talents."

We were silent for a beat before an idea began to take shape—an idea so wildly inappropriate, so utterly villainous, I didn't know if I should give it air.

"Anyways," Mai said with a heavy sigh. "I should get back to work."

The resignation in her tone fucking broke me.

"Wait." I turned, beginning to pace up and down the sidewalk. "I have an idea. What if we pretend?"

"Pretend?" Mai repeated. "Pretend what?"

"To be a couple."

Silence met my proposal. I held my phone away from my ear, checking the connection.

"Hello? Mai? You there?"

She cleared her throat. "Are you high?"

I snorted. "I wish."

"We can't pretend."

"Sure, we can." I moved to sit down but sprung back up, too filled with adrenaline. "You're single, I'm single. People know we hang out. Why not capitalize on that and just stretch the truth for a bit?"

"Are you seriously suggesting we manufacture a fake-dating situation?"

I shrugged. "Why not? People do it all the time to get on TV. And it's not like it's a lie."

"Except we're not dating."

"Well, we're not-not dating. Right?" I waved my hand around, frightening a rogue seagull. "I mean, we have joked that we're each other's platonic life partners more than once."

"That's a *joke*."

"Please?" I begged. "It'll be fun."

She let out a strangled bark of laughter. "You're seriously suggesting this?"

I sobered, running a hand through my hair. "You have

potential, Mai. You have an opportunity to win this. Sure, taking me along is a risk cause God knows I'm going to fuck things up for you. But at least we can say we tried."

"You can't even cut straight!"

I winced. "Filming doesn't start for another two weeks. We have time to practice and lay down the basics."

"The basics." She made a sound a little like a dying goose. "This is going be a disaster."

"Come on," I coaxed. "You know you want this."

I heard her hiccupping laugh, and my chest ached.

"More than I ever thought," she admitted, her voice low. "But us as a couple? I don't know if I want to lie."

I stared out at the shimmering blue-green water of the bay, listening to the gulls screech as a cool breeze touched my cheeks.

"Well then we find someone else." I said, trying to sound reasonable. "Someone you've dated who's into fashion. Or, at the very least, who can sew without requiring surgery."

My suggestion—while valid—felt wrong. My jaw clenched as I imagined someone else being with Mai, supporting her, laughing with her, pretending to be a couple.

What the fuck? This is Mai. Your friend. Remember?

I rolled my shoulders, trying to throw off the tension that had settled there.

"No. If we're going to do this—and I'm not saying we are. Then you're it." She cleared her throat. "Besides, having you there will help. You know how to talk me out of my panic."

My jealousy dissipated as concern flooded in.

"Are you struggling now?"

"No, I've already dealt with the worst of it."

Double fuck.

As much as I wanted her to agree to this crazy scheme, I needed to put Mai first.

"We don't have to do this if you feel uncomfortable."

I heard her moving around as she weighed my proposal. "I can't believe I'm about to say yes to you."

I chuckled softly. "So you're in."

She swore under her breath. "God help us, I'm in. But Theo?"

"Mm?"

"Consider this *your* challenge. Stepping outside your comfort zone and all that shit."

It seemed the Sakamoto siblings were determined to remind me of my many impulsive decisions.

"Whose idea was that anyway?"

"Yours."

I made a sound of disgust. "Remind me to never have a bright idea again. Alright, when do we begin?"

"Tonight?"

I thought of all the things I needed to do to make this happen.

"Tonight," I agreed, beginning to make a mental list. "Let's win you a million dollars."

"It's only two hundred and fifty thousand."

"Not if we take it to a casino and bet it all on black, *bay-bee.*"

She clucked her tongue. "Goodbye, Theo."

I was gratified to hear that some of the panic had eased from her voice.

"Later, Mai."

I hit end and stared blankly at my phone, my gaze unfocussed.

Fuck. What the hell did I get us into?

CHAPTER 4
THEO

I parked my car in the Garrett-Harris Paper lot, my hands flexing on the steering wheel. For the last ten-plus years, I'd worked as the head line supervisor, supporting my brother to bring the company back from the brink of insolvency.

It had been hard work turning around a failing business and making our paper products sustainable. Our father had driven the place into the ground before we'd taken it on, fighting to ensure our workers would still have jobs. When Annie Harris had bought into the business, I'd been apprehensive. There'd been a lot of dirt lying between my twin and his ex-girlfriend—most of it unresolved.

Thankfully, it had all worked out. The lucky bastard had won her over through grit and determination, and our business had thrived under their leadership. While I couldn't be happier for him—for them—I often felt like a third wheel in this partnership.

Making paper products hadn't exactly been on the top ten things I'd do with my life list. Once upon a time, I'd planned to play ball at college, maybe try for the pros, and if that failed, I'd become an occupational therapist or something. Life had a way of fucking with your plans.

I'd spent the last decade of my life between these walls, working on the operations floor and supporting our staff. I'd been content with my life, resigned to the fact that while not glamourous or exciting, the work had purpose.

But lately, I'd felt a yearning to do something different. Exactly what, I had no idea.

"Let's get this over with," I muttered, climbing out of the car.

Had anyone ever asked what I wanted in life, most people might assume I'd request a new leg, or perhaps a million dollars.

Nope. All I wanted was to not be a twin.

Not because I didn't love my brother. Fuck, I'd lay down my life for the guy.

I just hated how fucking difficult it was seeing someone who looked like you, who had similar experiences and the exact same upbringing, get his shit together, fall in love, get married, have kids, and live his happily ever after.

He had the life I wanted—as a dedicated partner, with a fulfilling job, and a bundle of kids—and it sucked ass watching a guy who had your face present you with a play-by-play of everything your heart desired. Seeing him with Annie and the kids made me feel like a voyeur to a life I could have—if only I tried harder or made better choices.

There were seven billion people in this world, and I had yet to meet one person who cared enough to want to settle down with me.

Maybe I was the problem.

"Fuck, get it together, Garrett." I shoved through the doors of the office building, calling greetings as I headed toward our shared office.

Our tired and worn gray office had been transformed into a colorful, warm space. There was life in these walls, people wanted to work here and enjoyed being involved with the growth of the company. I could take credit for some but not all of it. Most should be attributed to Annie and Linc, who'd put in the hard work and made the connections to drag us kicking and screaming from the dark ages.

But if anyone asked, I'd own the glory. After all, isn't that what younger brothers are meant to do? Ride on the coattails of their older sibling.

I shoved through the office door only to be greeted by a cacophony of naked limbs.

I should have knocked first.

"Jesus!" I smacked a hand over my poor abused eyes,

twirling to give my brother and his wife some privacy. "Again?"

I heard them scrambling for their clothes, knocking shit off their desk and no doubt causing an absolute mess.

"Sorry!" Annie called, sounding unsurprisingly unapologetic. "It's just—"

"You're trying for baby number three, I *know*."

God did I know. The two of them were like horny rabbits. Give 'em half a second alone and they were humping like their lives depended on it.

Though, I guess in the scheme of creating another human, one potential life did depend on their rumpy-pumpy action. Still, I didn't need to be treated to an X-rated peep show every five minutes.

I opened my fingers a fraction, twisting to see if they'd put themselves to right. "I thought we agreed the office would be a sex-free zone."

"I don't remember agreeing to that," Linc muttered, stuffing his shirt into his jeans. "Pretty sure I'd have remembered that being added to the employee handbook."

"It's under page three." I reached out to pull the manual from our office bookshelf and tossed it at him. "Right under the workplace health and safety standards."

Linc caught the book, placing it on his desk. "We should probably remove it. Or at least add an addendum that the ban only applies to the warehouse and break room." He leaned in to kiss Annie. "God knows I can't afford another write up."

"Don't like the way you're punished?" Annie asked, laying a hand on his chest. "You didn't have any complaints last—"

"Enough!" I stuck my fingers in my ear, making a la-la-la sound.

Annie tossed her mass of golden hair, laughing. She reminded me of a starlet from the early years of Hollywood —full-bodied and glowing. While she lived with Crohn's disease, in the last year she'd switched up her medication, and the change had given her more pain-free days and more energy. She practically vibrated with verve these days, and I loved that for her.

Annie flicked me the finger. "I've gotta get home anyway." She blew a kiss at Linc. "Don't stay too late."

She leaned in to kiss me, but I screwed up my face, shoving her away gently. "Don't touch me with those sex-stained lips, lady! You might be my favorite sister-in-law, but that doesn't give you the right to be spreading your sex germs all over the place."

Laughing, she flicked the side of my head with her finger. "You're terrible."

"But you still love me."

"Occasionally."

She blew a final kiss to Linc and left, leaving me to watch my brother watch his wife walk away with a tiny love-struck smile.

"Dude." I shook my head. "You've been married for three years. You have kids. Shouldn't you be over fucking-like-rabbits by now? Surely, you're moving into the quickie-missionary-while-the-kids-are-watching-cartoons-on-a-Sunday stage?"

"God forbid." Linc perched on the edge of my desk. "Isn't today your day off?"

"Mm."

An electric shock pulsed up the damaged nerves of my amputated limb. The false flag signals indicated I had a cramp in my non-existent calf.

Again?

Phantom pain had become a familiar part of my life. It varied between shooting and burning pains, to full-on cramps. I'd never tell anyone but my therapist, but I sometimes imagined it as a ghost limb, following me around like a specter, desperately trying to reattach itself and reclaim the life it should have had.

Not at all morbid.

Well used to the sensation, I began the process of removing my prosthetic, gritting my teeth against the pain.

"You okay?"

"Cramp," I managed to bite out. "It'll pass."

Linc reached over my desk, pulling a wheat bag from the top drawer of Annie's desk. "I'll get this. You need some pain relief?"

I shook my head.

In my last year of high school, I'd made the mistake of accepting a ride from our dad. Walter wasn't the kind of guy one could rely on. Drunk and a little high, he'd driven us straight into a power pole. The bastard had walked out practically unscathed while I'd lost my right lower limb. Ending at the knee, the leg was the one major difference in appearance between my twin and me.

Not so identical.

The incident changed the trajectory of my life. Medical bills, hospital costs, therapy, not to mention the changes that were required to my house to make it functional. The life I thought I'd have, the life I'd wanted to live, had been taken away.

I'd long ago made peace with my reality, but that didn't mean that I didn't grieve. There is a grief that comes with knowing there are paths of your life that you'll never walk. You can mourn the dreams you had for yourself, and the experiences you envisioned that won't be achieved, while still finding joy in the decisions you choose to pursue.

Fuck me, I'm a morose bastard today.

Well used to my occasional muscle spasms, Linc returned with the warmed heat pack, handing it to me to lay over my rigid, throbbing muscles.

"Thanks." I dug my thumbs into the spasming tissue. "I need to talk to you."

Linc settled against my desk, his expression carefully blank. "Shoot."

I knew that expression. I despised it.

It was his, I-want-to-help-make-everything-better-but-I-know-better-than-to-offer look. It was the worst, second only to his, I-wish-it-had-been-me-in-that-car look. He tried to hide it but was never quite successful.

"I need to take some leave."

Linc's eyebrows rose. "Okay, when were you thinking?"

"Two weeks."

"Uh-huh. And for how long?"

This would be the true test of our relationship. "At least six weeks."

"What?" Linc spluttered. "Six weeks?"

I sighed silently. Dropping my head, I watched my thumbs massage my flesh. "Mai needs help with something. I said I'd do it."

"For six weeks?"

"I know it's asking a lot—"

Linc snorted.

"—especially at short notice. But I promised her."

He crossed his arms over his chest. "What *exactly* did you promise?"

Heat crept up my neck as I muttered my response.

"Sorry? I didn't catch that."

I cleared my throat. "We're going on a reality TV show."

"Like a singles show or something?"

I rolled my eyes. "Jesus, I'm not that desperate."

"I beg to differ. How many dates have you been on this year?"

I shrugged. "One has to kiss a lot of...." I paused, trying to think of a polite alternative to the gross use of an amphibious creature. "Friends before finding their forever."

"If not a dating show, then what?"

I hesitated. "A game show."

"Like trivia?"

"Kind of?"

"An adventure game show?"

I cringed. "Not quite."

He narrowed his eyes. "Theodore, you're being deliberately obtuse."

"You know I fucking hate that name."

"Then tell me exactly what you've signed up for."

"It's a fashion show." I swallowed hard, bracing myself for the forthcoming roasting.

For a beat my brother stared at me, his face stupefied.

He shook his head as if to clear it. "Sorry, I must have passed out. Did you say *fashion*?"

I nodded, wincing.

"And you'll be Mai's—what? Apprentice? Helper?"

I shrugged, not wanting to go too much into the details. "Something like that."

"She knows you can't sew, right?"

"I can too," I responded, aware I sounded like a petulant toddler.

"You were in the hospital getting stitches last week."

"Well, I can knit."

Linc snorted. "Unless you're asked to knit a whole-body scarf condom, I'm doubtful you'll be of much assistance."

"You make one Christmas gift...."

Linc pinched the bridge of his nose. "You're sure you want to do this?"

"Absolutely not," I replied cheerfully. "But Mai needs me." The cramping in my leg eased, the heat of the wheat pack calming the frantic muscles. I leaned back in my seat. "And I promised."

"I still find it strange she asked you. Why not Flo or Frankie or Annie?"

I didn't feel comfortable telling him about my new loved-up status without first speaking to Mai. I wanted to protect her from the scrutiny our fake relationship would bring for as long as possible.

I held up my hand, ticking off the short list of names on my fingers. "Flo doesn't sew and has her own business. Annie has the twins and you, not to mention this." I waved a hand around to encompass our office.

"There's still Frankie."

I snorted. "Frankie is an awesome individual, don't get me wrong. But she also has her own business, clients, her podcast, and TV show, and do you really think Jay would let her go away for six weeks to a place where he can't reach her? This is a no-contact situation."

Linc shrugged. "If the guy thought Mai needed her, sure."

"Well, she asked me." I crossed my arms over my chest.

"Doesn't she want to win?"

Buddy, you have no idea.

"I assume so." I spread my arms out. "And who says I can't be useful?"

Linc's eyebrows rose. "Have you ever made anything?"

"There was that one shirt."

"If memory serves, didn't it disintegrate on the first wear?"

I waved my hand dismissively. "It was meant to do that. I like to call it recyclable fashion. You get to reuse the fabric and turn it into something new after every wear."

"Uh-huh," Linc said, looking utterly unconvinced. "That explains why it fell apart mid-dinner."

I shrugged. "Prototypes always have some kinks to work out."

"You're determined to do this?"

I nodded.

"Well, fuck." He ran a hand through his hair. "Guess I better see about replacing you."

My tension eased. "You sure?"

"No. But I'm gonna do it anyway because I love your annoying ass, and you haven't asked for a day off in three years. You took on the bulk of operations for the business after the twins were born, and I appreciate that. The least I could do is support you to do whatever the fuck it is you think you're doing."

I chuckled. "Look I didn't say it was a good idea. I expect we'll be eliminated the first week, but either way, I have to try."

"Have to or want to?"

I shrugged. "Mai asked, so I'm gonna do it."

Linc crossed his arms over his chest, his gaze considering. "It's like that, is it?"

Jesus, what was it with people wanting to drill down on my relationships today?

"I would ask 'like what' but" —I stood, tossing him the heat pack—"I gotta get going. There's a lot to organize before I leave for God only knows where."

"You've applied for leave, and you know I'll look after the house. What else is there?"

"I need to learn how to fucking sew."

My brother laughed but halted me as I reached the door.

"Theo, wait."

I glanced back, hovering in the doorway.

Linc ran a hand through his hair. "This is gonna sound shit but... while you're away, take some time to think about what you want." He gestured to the office around us. "This has become my dream—and it's for sure Annie's. I know you're invested, but I also know you're not happy. We're in a good place now. I want you to be in a good place too."

I forced out a rusty laugh. "Trying to kick me out?"

He didn't even smile. "Never. I know you. This isn't your dream. And that's okay if this is just a means to an end

—like if your dream is traveling or buying a house or blowing all your hard-earned cash at the casino—don't do that though. Please."

I leaned against the doorway, waiting for him to finish.

"The point is, I think you've lost sight of what you want. I want you to—between all the filming—take some time to work out what you want." He paused. "And look, if that's leaving here and doing something different, then shit, we'll miss you, but you need to do something that will make you happy. You've sacrificed enough."

I jerked up my chin, silently acknowledging his words.

"Okay, get out of here." He waved me off. "I need to rewrite the staff handbook."

I hesitated. "Linc?"

He glanced up.

"Thanks." I swallowed the lump in my throat. "I know that was hard to say. But I appreciate it."

"Love you, bro."

"Love you too." I sighed dramatically, needing to lighten the mood. "I always knew you were the emotional one."

He chuckled. "Get out of here. I have work to do."

I drove home and pulled into the driveway of my rental, and sat in the car, staring at the faded weatherboard bungalow.

Linc's words had struck a chord, unearthing a yearning question.

What do I want?

The unknown hung heavy in the air, frustratingly unreachable.

"You have time to work it out," I reassured myself. "All the time in the world."

I exited the car, hunching my shoulders against the cool afternoon breeze as it stirred the leaves that were just beginning to turn yellow. Soon, pumpkins and ghouls would appear, followed by mangers filled with apples—an old Astipia tradition that harked back to a time when farmers shared their harvest.

A floorboard creaked under my foot as I stepped into the house and closed my door, sealing myself inside the dim interior.

I'd moved into the bungalow when Linc and Annie had gotten serious. The temporary rental had been a place to pause until I found a better option—but somehow it had turned into a long-term arrangement.

Old furniture clashed with new purchases and peeling paint, dodgy floorboards, and threadbare rugs.

Was this really the life I wanted? Going through the motions with no passion?

"Fuck." I closed my eyes. "Linc might be right."

At some point, I'd lost sight of my dreams and desires. I'd put myself into a holding pattern.

My phone vibrated with an incoming text.

I pulled it from my pocket, swiping at the screen.

MAI

Distract me from my fear and doubts by brainstorming team names. I'll start. I'm in favor of "Sew Good"

Chuckling, I hit reply.

THEO

How about "Stitched up"?

I smiled wryly, awaiting her response. This whole thing felt like a disaster just waiting to happen—and yet, I had a suspicion it might be exactly what I needed to break out of the monotonous routine I'd fallen into. Sure, I had no idea what the fuck I was doing, but somehow that made it even more appealing. The thought of diving into something so far outside my comfort zone felt good.

Mai's reply didn't disappoint.

MAI

Haute Mess Express

Chuckling, I shot back another response.

THEO

Seam Dream Team

MAI

The Unthreadables

Ready to out-pun her, I kicked off my shoe and flopped onto my couch, pleased to find the restless feeling Linc had stirred up had settled—at least for now.

CHAPTER 5
MAI

I placed a tray of tea and snacks on my coffee table, then crossed to the small sewing area I'd set up years before. Hunched over the humming machine, Theo diligently fed the fabric through the needle, attempting to complete the hem of a shirt for what felt like the millionth time.

We'd spent the last week holed up in my apartment, teaching him the basics of fashion design. It was going... slowly.

"Ah ha!" he declared, releasing his foot from the pedal to stop the machine. "We have success."

He snipped some loose threads and flicked the shirt out with a showman's flourish before handing it to me.

I examined his work, trying not to smile as he fidgeted in place, awaiting my judgment.

"This hemline is looking more like a seismic graph than a straight line," I teased, holding up the lopsided fabric. "But I can see improvement."

He made a wounded animal sound clutching at his chest. "Come on. You gotta admit it's not bad for a guy with one leg."

I snorted. "Because your leg impacts your ability to follow a straight line."

"Exactly." He nodded, plucking the shirt from my hands. "I'm glad you understand."

He pulled a seam ripper from the back pocket of his jeans and began to unpick each thread. His fingers moved deftly, surprisingly sure and agile for guy who'd only just begun to understand the basics of sewing.

"Getting good at this," he said with a grin. "Perhaps you

could employ me as your lead seam ripper." He held up the small tool, pretending to call to an audience. "Seam ripper! Seam ripper! Forty bucks a seam!"

"It says a lot about you that destruction is your favorite part of the creative process."

With the seam disassembled, he reached for a small pincushion full of needles, his fingers moving quickly to re-pin the fabric.

"What rating this time?" he asked with a grin.

"I give you a D plus," I responded, straight-faced, though laughter threatened to bubble up my throat. "But an A plus for effort and enthusiasm."

"I thank you for the crumbs from your table. I—ouch!" He winced, sticking his fingertip in his mouth to suck at the pin prick. "For the record, when I signed up for this gig, you failed to mention anything about blood pacts."

"Think of it as a hazard of the job." I nudged him playfully with my elbow as I leaned in to inspect his work. "You're doing really well, Theo. Seriously. I couldn't have asked for a better...." I paused, unsure of how to describe our fake relationship.

"Partner in crime?" he asked cheekily.

The apprehension, guilt, and panic began to breakthrough the opaque barrier I'd erected, oozing into my stomach and slithering up my spine.

"We still have time," I whispered, all sense of lightness disappearing under the avalanche of stress that threatened to overwhelm me. "We could just call them and say we've made a mistake. That we broke up or that we—"

"Shhh," Theo hushed, stepping away from the sewing

area to wrap me in a warm, tight hug. "We've got this. I promise. No one's going know that we're faking it. No one's going to even suspect this isn't real. You're going on that show, you're going to do your best, and that's all anyone could ask."

I closed my eyes, letting him hold me for a long moment as I listened to the steady beat of his heart against my ear. I took comfort in the warmth his skin radiated against mine.

My brother and Theo had been friends for years—ever since Ren had returned to the Cove upon graduation from the academy. My brother had only ever wanted to be a firefighter, and his graduation and placement back in the Cove had been a source of great joy and pride for my family.

And not a small amount of relief to my *haha*, who had worried over my brother since the day she'd brought him into the world. As her eldest child—and only boy—Ren had paved the path for my sister and I to follow our dreams. But he'd also left a chaotic mess in his wake, bringing others along with him for the ride.

Looking back, I still wasn't sure exactly how Theo had managed to wiggle his way into my life. One second, we'd been kind-of acquaintances, and the next we were fake dating.

I am bamboozled by this relationship.

As much as I loved my friends—and Annie, Frankie, and Flo were as closer to me than my own sister—I had to admit that what Theo and I had was different. Somehow, he'd stormed past my defenses to become an essential part of my life.

Theo adjusted his hold on me, recognizing that I needed to be held more than I needed him to let go—despite how awkwardly long this hug had become.

But then, that's who he was. Theo just happened to be the type of guy who felt the best way to support someone was with a kind word and a gentle gesture. Unlike many of the men in my life, he had no apprehension in offering physical touch—understanding the comfort that came from a tangible connection.

I couldn't help but admire his determination to be a source of positivity in a world that seemed determined to be negative. That he had directed his attention and friendship toward me would forever remain a source of confusion.

The longer he held me, the more aware I became of how tight his arms banded around my body. He smelled intoxicating and soothing all at once, the scent of his cologne tickling my nose. His fingers were splayed, one hand cupping the back of my head, the other pressing against my back to cradle me to his chest. His fingers at my nape absentmindedly played in my hair, gently stroking through the strands.

Goose bumps rose on my arms as my stomach gave a little flip.

Uh-oh.

I blinked, stiffening as my body reacted to his closeness.

Oh no!

At some point, Theo had become an essential part of my life. And if my reaction was anything to go by, it appeared that I was nursing a crush on a guy who only offered friendship.

Such was my life.

I released him and stepped back. "Sorry. I didn't mean to do that."

Theo gently tucked my hair back behind my ear, the gesture sweet but caring.

"I did." He dipped slightly to catch my embarrassed gaze, his eyes warm and full of understanding. "I'm a good cuddler."

Therein lay the crux of my issues. Because Theo Garrett wasn't a "good" cuddler. Theo Garrett was a world-class cuddler. If cuddling was an extreme sport, Theo would be the world champion.

As a person who'd grown up in a loving and supportive, but touch-restrained, family, his kind of freely given physical affection really strained the boundaries of our relationship—at least in my own mind.

Honestly, how could anyone resist such a man?

"How about we try teaching you how to measure a live person?" I changed the subject, needing to shift us from the slightly flirty place to which we'd navigated, back to safe waters.

He tilted his head to one side. "Is it very different to measuring the road test dummy?"

"The adjustable mannequin," I corrected. "And yeah, it really is. Precision is key." I laced my voice with mock severity as I picked up a soft measuring tape. His eyes locked on to mine for a moment, and I felt that familiar flutter in my chest—the one I refused to identify.

Don't do it to yourself, Mai.

"Right, precision," he echoed, clearing his throat while unfolding the tape. "Where do I start?"

"You need to ask the model a few questions—like to stand naturally, upright and with feet hip-width apart." I demonstrated. "Next, you check their clothing." I gestured to his plaid overshirt. "If they're wearing layers, get them to remove the outer garment. You don't want to be creating something that will be too big because they're wearing a puffer jacket."

He chuckled. "No puffer jackets—got it."

"If they're female, check if they're wearing the same bra that they will be with the end product." I gestured at my breasts. "Cup sizes can make or break an outfit."

His gaze dipped to my chest, and I swear I saw him swallow. He turned his head away, a slight flush touching his cheeks. "Noted."

"Theo," I said slowly, delighted I'd managed to unsettle him. "Are you worried about being near my boobs?"

His blush deepened. "Not at all. I'm just worried about *you* worrying about *me* being near your boobs."

"Nawww." I lifted some plain marking tape from the table. "Come learn how to measure a living person before you lose your nerve."

I instructed him on how to wrap the tape around my waist, which would help him to take length measurements down or up to the same point.

"Now," I instructed after he'd tied the tape around my waist, "we measure my neck."

I showed him how to place the measuring tape around my neck, laying the plastic flat against the dip in my collarbone.

"See?" I asked, demonstrating. "This is the measurement you want to capture."

He nodded, his gaze narrowing as he observed my movements.

"Next we do the shoulders." I stepped closer, tilting my body so he could see how I laid the tape across my shoulders.

"We measure from the collarbone across to the end of the collarbone, here." I pulled the neckline of my shirt away to show where the knobby part of my shoulder ended. "Generally, you measure on both sides then average it to get the shoulder numbers."

"Generally? When would you not do that?"

"If someone has one arm larger than the other or has a disability. You want to make sure that the fit is comfortable for them."

Theo nodded.

I ran him through the other areas, showing him how to measure my breasts, waists, hips, thighs, and other areas.

"Okay." I handed him the measuring tape. "Your turn."

I rolled my shoulders back and turned to face him more fully. He gripped the tape, his quiet inhale brushing my hair as he leaned in.

The tape took on a different feel as he laid it gently against my skin. His fingers were warm as he manipulated it to take the first measurement.

"Like this?" he asked.

"Perfect," I murmured.

He hummed to himself as he moved to my shoulder. The tape slid across one shoulder, then the other, as Theo asked me to turn this way or that.

"Next, bust," I said, trying to sound professional as he finished recording the number.

I tried to ignore the heat crawling up my neck when his hands hovered inches from my body. He met my eyes briefly, a question lingering in his gaze. I swallowed hard, gesturing for him to continue.

"Sorry if this is awkward," he murmured as the tape encircled me at chest level. His knuckles brushed lightly against my sides, sparking a trail of goose bumps along my skin.

As he moved from measurement to measurement, my thoughts became a jumble of scattered pieces. My attention narrowed to where his hands touched my body, where the tape rasped across my clothes, where his breath brushed against my skin.

He pulled a chair closer to sit in as he began to measure my lower body.

"Easier than crouching," he murmured, nodding his head toward his prosthetic.

I nodded, unable to speak as a coil of tension wound tight in my middle. Leaning forward, Theo frowned a little as he began to measure.

The heat of his hands penetrated the thin fabric of my leggings, his touch gentle as he wrapped the tape around my thigh.

"Like this?" he asked, glancing up.

"Uh, yeah." Our gazes held for a long beat, something unexpected passing between us.

This is Theo. You're not interested in Theo, remember?

I watched his Adam's apple bob before he dipped his head, continuing with his measurements.

"Calves next," I murmured, hyperaware of Theo being so near to my abdomen.

He nodded once, leaning further forward in his seat to reach my lower legs.

The gentle rasp of the tape and our breathing were the only sounds in the silence of the room.

"I think I'm done."

I let out a breath I hadn't realized I'd been holding, feeling a little wobbly as I stepped back.

"You did great." The words felt far too benign when compared to the aching tension he'd managed to build. I turned away, clearing my throat. "There are snacks on the coffee table."

He perked up. "What kind of snacks?"

"Does it matter?" I asked lightly, striving to navigate us back to familiar waters. "We both know you'll eat anything."

He chuckled, following me across to the low table. "True. But I'm always wary after you fed me those wasabi peas."

I groaned, settling into a *seiza* position beside the low table. "I get you to try one new thing and you hold that over me for years."

He made a face as he sat cross-legged on the other side of the table. "I don't think I've cried that much since Astipia lost to Spain in the Football World Cup."

I snorted, lifting the small teapot from the tray. "You cried that much in the kids' movie we watched the other week."

"Hey! So did you!"

I poured us some green tea. "Ignoring our mutual angst over animated characters, we should talk about what happens tomorrow."

"Before we do that." He leaned over, stretching his long body until he could hook a finger into the strap of his bag. Dragging it across the floor, he rummaged inside until he could pull a small gift bag free.

"This is for you," he said, placing it on the table.

I finished pouring and handed him his cup. "What is it?"

"A present."

I inclined my head toward the coffee table. "You already brought me grapes."

Theo had once asked why Ren and I brought gifts when we came to his house. I'd explained that gift-giving is a tradition in Japanese culture, and that gifts are often used to express gratitude or care.

Once I'd explained the significance, Theo had then adopted the custom, surprising me each time he came over with small gifts like fruit, cookies or tea.

The practice of *temiyage,* had been drilled into my siblings and I from a young age. My *obaachan* had lived with us for most of my younger years until we'd moved to the Cove. She'd moved to Astipia as a young bride with my *ojiisan.*

She'd spoken only rudimentary English at the time and had struggled to find work to sustain her. It was through the diaspora community that she'd met other skilled seamstresses, becoming good friends with many of the women. Together, they'd established a small store for mending, tailoring and the occasional design, until she'd retired many years ago. She'd been my first teacher and had encouraged my love of design.

Theo lifted the mug in both of his hands, blowing

gently on the hot liquid, sending steam swirling gently across his face. "This is different." He nodded at the gift bag. "Open it."

I reached for the bag, feeling slightly self-conscious as I rifled through the gift.

"I know you're nervous about this," Theo explained as I withdrew a fluffy brown unicorn. "I thought this might help."

The stuffed toy stared up at me with gentle brown eyes. Urma the unicorn has been my favorite adults' cartoon for years—the snarky, foulmouthed equine always made me laugh.

"Thank you."

Theo reached for a cookie with a shrug. "There's more."

I smoothed the soft fur of the unicorn and put it aside, reaching in to withdraw a small candle. The label branded it as being created by my friend Flo, who owned "Common Scents." She made everything from candles to perfumes to oils, each tailored to the individual's preference.

Gently pulling the lid off, I drew in a deep breath, inhaling the scent of salt and wind.

"I had Flo design it for you," Theo explained around a mouthful of sweets. "To remind you of home if you get homesick when we're away."

A warm, aching feeling radiated from my chest. "This is very thoughtful. You shouldn't have."

He ignored me, reaching for another cookie.

I tipped the bag and two small packages fell out—one a gorgeous box, the other a small, hand-wrapped circle.

I opened the lid of the box, my breath catching. Inside

nestled between silky pieces of fabric sat a small gold ring. On the ring sat the kanji for person, 人.

"I read about *hito wo nomu*," Theo explained, leaning over to touch the ring. "Though I'm sure I butchered that pronunciation. I thought I'd get the symbol made into a ring so when you're nervous you can look it and hopefully feel calmer."

An old Japanese tradition, the idea was that when nervous in front of an audience, you wrote *hito*, 人, three times on the palm of your hand with one finger and then swallowed it, which would help you feel calmer.

"Shit, is that inappropriate?" Theo shifted in his seat. "I thought because you can't always spare a hand when you're busy, but you can always glance at it and think about—fuck. Sorry."

A lump formed in my throat at his thoughtfulness.

I shook my head, slipping the ring on my middle finger. "It's lovely, Theo. It's a beautiful, meaningful gift."

He relaxed, a small grin pulling at lips. "I'm glad it fits. Now open the last one, this is my favorite."

I cleared my throat. "That doesn't bode well." I tugged off the paper and pulled the small wrist pincushion free. A photo of his laughing face took up the entirety of the surface cushion.

"Theo!"

He chuckled. "Now when I annoy you, you can prick me instead of yelling at me."

I slipped it on my wrist, laughing. "You're ridiculous."

"But you like me anyway."

"I've been brainwashed," I agreed, lifting my cup of tea. "Thank you for the gifts."

"Anytime." He shifted, his grin lingering. "Now, let's talk about what happens when we get to the studio."

I nodded, my heart rate kicking up as my amusement faded. "If we're going to...." I couldn't bring myself to say the word.

"Stretch the truth?" Theo asked, tilting his head to one side.

"Sure, let's go with that." I swirled my cup absently, taking comfort in the familiar warmth of the ceramic in my hands. "We should ensure we're clear on our origin story."

"Not to mention boundaries."

"Boundaries?"

Theo nodded. "You know, touching, kissing, that kind of thing."

I blinked rapidly. "You think they'll want us to kiss?" My gaze flicked to his lips, then darted away, a small flush creeping up my neck.

I couldn't deny I'd imagined kissing Theo once or twice. Okay, maybe a few more times than that. But it didn't mean anything. It was a natural reaction to having known someone so long. You wondered things about them. Like if they kissed hard or soft. If they enjoyed tongue or lip-nibbling teases.

You know, the normal stuff one wondered about their friends.

"Babe...." He seemed to be fighting a grin. "This is a couples competition. Of course, they're going to want us to kiss."

I blanched, feeling the blood drain from my face. "But... but...." I swallowed rapidly. "But we're not—that is—I mean—"

Kissing Theo? Thinking about it felt completely different to considering the actual act. I mean, what if I liked it? What if it changed things between us? What if—

Theo butt shuffled around the table until he was seated beside me. Wrapping an arm around my shoulders, he squeezed tight.

"Don't overthink this. Breathe."

I did as told, but it felt like a blockage had been put in place at the top of my lungs, preventing the air from reaching my chest.

I hadn't had enough time to consider all the possible outcomes of kissing Theo. I mean, I had in a theoretical sense considered it at some point—because hello anxiety. But pushing this all on me right now felt overwhelming. I needed time to think about what this would do to our relationship. Who we would be after we kissed. What would happen next.

I wheezed, panic constricting my chest.

"Slower," Theo coaxed, his voice soft and low. "With me."

He caught my hand and pressed it above his heart. The solid, even thud under my palm felt reassuring as his chest rose with one long breath. Theo held it for a beat of four before letting it out slowly.

I followed him, hating that I needed his guidance in how to do something every human on this Earth knew how to do since birth. Anger, frustration, and embarrassment swirled as I tried to do what my psychologist had taught me—to detach my thoughts from the emotion.

"You can observe your reactions and emotions without judgment, Mai," she'd told me. "There is no need to be afraid or apologetic about what you're feeling. Anxiety and panic have kept us alive for centuries. Acknowledge them and let it pass."

'Twas easier said than done.

"Are you sure Linc is okay with you taking six weeks?" I asked, trying to distract myself.

Theo nodded. "Now that Garrett-Harris Paper has evolved into a thriving enterprise, I'm all but superfluous to their needs."

I forced a laugh out of my dry mouth. "That's a sixteen-point word in scrabble."

He chuckled. "Little nerd. What I mean is, I'm not really sure why I'm even still there." A strange look crossed his face, something vulnerable and uncertain, before he wiped it away behind a mask of good cheer.

"Don't do that."

His eyebrows rose. "Do what?"

"Hide your uncertainty." I gestured between us. "If you have my back, let me have yours."

"I don't want to burden you with my insecurities."

I reared back. "Is that how you see me? As a burden?"

"What? Fuck no."

I swallowed. "Then why not let me help?" I practically read his mind as he opened his mouth, then snapped it shut. "God forbid, Theo. You better not have been about to say, 'but this is different.'"

He had the decency to look ashamed. "It... kind of is?"

"No, it's not."

He sighed, pushing up from the ground to shuffle around my living room. His movements were awkward, twitchy. He seemed to need to move to process the uncertainty that had settled on his shoulders.

"I don't love my job." I could hear the apprehension in his voice. "And yet, I can't see myself working anywhere else. I don't have the drive to go to university, don't have a burning desire or dream to fulfill, I'm just...." He shrugged. "Floating."

The hairs on the back of my neck stood up. There was something about the way he said "floating" that worried me.

"Are you okay?"

His lips tilted up, but his smile didn't reach his eyes. "Let's concentrate on your dreams and getting through the next six weeks before we worry about me."

I wanted to protest, but the words slipped away from me when I saw the guarded expression on his face. Experience had taught me that Theo rarely enjoyed revealing aspects of his life before he felt emotionally ready to dig into an issue. If I pushed, he'd deflect with humor.

Respecting his request, I nodded, tucking our conversation away for further exploration when he was ready to do so.

"Good." He made a move to sit back down beside me, but instead, awkwardly rolled on his prosthetic, tripping onto my couch.

I bit my tongue to keep from checking on him, already knowing Theo would hate me fussing.

"Pass me those cookies?" he asked, gesturing at the plate as if the trip had never happened.

Wordlessly, I obeyed.

"So," he said, munching happily. "What's our play?"

I sipped my tea, thinking. "The closer we stick to our truth, the easier it will be to maintain the lie."

"Right." He nodded, passing me a cookie. "I approached you about a cake, fell in love with your cooking and then your personality." He winked. "They do say the way to a man's heart is through his stomach."

I groaned, tossing a small throw pillow at him. "Please don't say that on camera."

"Too late, it's in my pun box."

I shifted to sit cross-legged on the floor, leaning back against the couch behind me. "What was our first date?"

He tilted his head back in thought. "That time we went to the roller derby, and I ended up having to break up the fight between the two women after the game."

I snorted with laughter. "Oh God! Your black eye!"

He winced, touching his left brow as if the pain remained. "She must have been a professional boxer. She had quite the right hook."

"She did apologize."

"Yeah. Didn't make my eye feel any better though."

We exchanged a grin.

"Okay. So that puts our relationship at...." I mentally did the sums. "Wow. Nearly four years."

"Has it really been that long since Frankie's wedding?"

I gestured at the photo that hung on my wall. Frankie wore a magnificent wedding dress that fit perfectly with her pink wheelchair. Her husband, Jay, sat in her lap, his arms around her shoulders as they laughed at the camera. Behind them stood our friendship group in various stages of laughter. I wore a crimson silk dress that I'd created and had my arm draped over Flo's shoulder. Flo's blonde hair had been decorated with a flower crown, and when paired with her blue flowing dress, it made her look like a bohemian pixie. At her side stood her yellow Labrador guide dog, Ace, looking dapper in a smart bowtie. Annie stood beside me, all golden skin and sensual curves.

That had been the night Linc had finally made a play for Annie—beginning to repair the relationship that had been broken between them.

"A lot has happened since then."

Theo nodded thoughtfully. "Yeah, I guess it has."

I cleared my throat. "I can't say that your dance moves have improved."

Theo laid a hand on his chest in mock outrage. "How dare you! I am a superb dancer."

"Sure. If one likes being slapped in the face by their dance partner."

"Some people are into that kind of thing."

We grinned at each other.

"Back to the issue at hand. What else do we need to confirm to make this relationship seem real?"

I tilted my head to one side, considering all the scenarios. "They might ask when we started designing together."

"That we can be honest about. A year later, and I'm still a mess."

My stress eased a little. "That's true. We'll be up against those who are likely ten times better than us."

"But we'll try our best. If nothing else, it'll be good exposure for you." He clapped a hand on my shoulder and squeezed. "I'll try not to hold you back."

A grateful lump formed in my throat. "You won't. We're in this together."

He made a rumbling sound. "Now on to the touchy-feely shit. What are we doing about PDAs?"

I clasped my hands together in my lap, surprised to find my palms had grown sweaty.

This is Theo, I reminded myself. *Nothing to be nervous about.*

"We should probably hold hands. Maybe an arm around the shoulder kind of thing."

His glance slid toward me, hesitating for just a moment too long. "What about kissing?"

My cheeks warmed. "M-maybe one or two. For authenticity."

"Right, authenticity."

We both glanced away, a weirdly uncomfortable silence falling.

"Should we... practice?" he asked, his voice strained. "You know, so it looks natural."

My heart kicked up, thumping heavily against my ribcage. "Um...."

"We don't have to," Theo rushed to assure me. "I mean... plenty of couples don't do PDAs."

He had to be right, but I just couldn't think of any off the top of my head.

"Like who?"

"Charles and Camilla?" he said, referring to the king and queen of England.

I snorted. "I don't think they count."

"Umm... there's bound to be others."

We stared at each other, then burst out laughing.

"We're hopeless."

He nodded. "That we are."

Our gazes locked, our amusement draining away.

Theo leaned in, his eyes trained on me, his jaw tense.

"Yes or no, Mai?"

I drew on my courage, nodding my head slightly at his question.

A small grin tipped up one corner of his mouth. He slid onto the floor beside me, moving into my space until I was pressed against the couch, Slowly, deliberately, he cupped my face, sliding his thumb across my bottom lip.

"I'm gonna need words."

My heart pounded in my chest, a tight shimmering ache beginning deep between my legs. I liked that he wanted verbal confirmation of my permission. I liked that he didn't just assume.

But fuck if it didn't make it ten times as hard to answer him.

Sucking in a deep breath, I locked eyes with him. Settling my hands on his chest, I gently tugged at his shirt, pulling him toward me.

"Ye—"

A knocking on my door interrupted us. We both jumped, springing apart as if we were teenagers caught making out on his parents' couch.

"Let us in!" Annie called from the other side. "We have wine!"

I closed my eyes, uncertain if I was grateful or annoyed by the interruption.

"Coming," I called. "Sorry, it's Red and Read night."

"Ah." Theo pushed up to a stand, then leaned down to help me stand. "I understand."

I walked with him to the door, trying to process the weird mix of disappointment and relief that the girls' interruption had stirred.

Theo put his hand to the doorknob, then paused.

"Fuck it," he murmured.

I opened my mouth to ask what he meant when he spun. His fingers wrapped around my elbow, drawing me in.

"Just once," he said, his voice strained. "Just to break the ice."

My breath hitched when his hand found the small of my back, drawing me close until our faces were inches apart.

"Ready?" he asked, searching my gaze.

"I...." I swallowed, my heart pounding so loud I was sure he could hear it. "I think so?"

"Say no." His lips tilted into a grin. "Or kiss me on the count of three. Ready? One."

"Two," I spluttered.

"Three."

His head dipped and paused a hairsbreadth above my lips—leaving me to close the gap between us.

Do it, an inner voice I didn't recognize encouraged. *Take what you want.*

I lifted on tiptoe, and our lips met in a soft, tentative kiss that stole the air from my lungs.

Oh, my heart seemed to sigh. *This is what we've been missing.*

At first, Theo kept the kiss light and easy, allowing me space to break away. But I didn't. A million thoughts flickered through my mind in the spaces between my heartbeats.

I should pull back.

I should kiss him harder.

I should... I should... I should.

He made the decision for me, stepping closer and adjusting the angle of our kiss. Heat washed over me, flooding my body as the kiss shifted from sweet and gentle, growing deeper, hungrier, filled with need.

Sensations assaulted me as his hand slid up my elbow to cup my neck, his thumb stroking my pulse point.

I opened my mouth, wanting to taste him.

"Mai! Open up!"

The amused shout interrupted us. We jumped away from each other, both of us flustered and blushing.

Theo cleared his throat and adjusted his clothing, his hand back on the doorknob.

"Well," he said, avoiding my gaze. "We know that's not going to be a problem."

A hysterical giggle bubbled up my throat and burst out of my mouth. I slapped a hand across my lips, staring at him wide-eyed as I tried to find some calm.

His lips twisted into a half smirk. "Good night, Mai."

"Night," I whispered, sobering.

His hand snaked out and he gently, if not awkwardly, patted my head before walking out the door.

"She's all yours, ladies," he said to my friends before speed-walking away.

Annie stared at me, her eyebrows raised.

"Excuse me," she said, tilting her head to one side as Theo left. "Why are you all flushed and sweaty?"

Flo jerked upright. "She's flushed and sweaty?"

I groaned, slapping a hand over my face. "This is a nightmare."

Frankie pushed through my door, wheeling toward my couch. "Get inside, we need to hear *all* about it."

Sighing heavily, I knew there would be no escaping their questions. Resigning myself to a night of interrogation, I pulled my cell from my pocket.

"Pizza?" I asked.

Annie eyed me as she took a seat on my couch. "You might want to put in an order for a six-pack, while you're at it."

How true her words were.

The best and worst thing about friends is how well they grew to know you. Sometimes I didn't need to say a word for them to know exactly what I wanted—be it chocolate, a hug, or space.

Other times, it sucked ass that you couldn't slip anything past them.

"We were just practicing," I repeated for the millionth time as we finished our dinner. "It meant nothing."

Annie pointed her pizza crust at me, her expression filled with scepticism. "Don't forget, I'm married to a Garrett twin. I know how those boys work. They suck you in with sweet words and gentle touches and before you know it, they're bending you over a table and fucking you pregnant."

I made a face. "Jesus, Annie! TMI!"

She waved a hand dismissively. "As if you haven't heard this before."

"Or seen it," Frankie muttered with a shudder.

"Hey, you're the ones who didn't knock."

"You were screaming like someone was murdering you!"

"He was," Annie agreed with a wide smirk. "With his dick."

Flo leaned into me, pressing her shoulder against mine. "The question you haven't answered—and the one in which I'm most interested—is how did you feel kissing him? You guys have been friends a long time. I know how your brain works. Is there any interest?"

As a person who identified as demisexual, I didn't experience sexual attraction until developing a close bond with someone. Primary sexual attraction—the kind a lot of people experienced upon first meeting someone—just didn't happen for me. I could appreciate a person's attractiveness objectively, but it wasn't until I knew them that I began to experience arousal.

Based on the way my body had responded to Theo— and the arousal still simmering through my blood hours later—it appeared I'd subconsciously moved him from friend to crush.

"I don't know," I groaned, slumping back in my seat to stare up at my ugly popcorn ceiling. "I'm confused."

Frankie knit her hands together under her chin. "What is your confusion stemming from?"

I shrugged. "I'm normally pretty good at identifying when I'm beginning to develop feelings for a friend. Tonight took me by surprise." I sighed. "I guess I'm confused if it's actual genuine feelings or if I'm just experiencing a physical reaction. It has been a while since...." I gestured to my crotch.

"You beat the bean?" Annie asked.

"Fed the kitty?" Frankie offered.

"Nulled the void?" Flo said, her voice strangled with amusement.

"I hate you all."

They burst out laughing.

Flo laid a hand on my knee. "Are you going to be okay to pull this charade off for the next six weeks?"

Ah, as always, she cut straight to the heart of the issue.

"I have to be," I said earnestly. "I want this opportunity. All it takes is one design that people love for your career to take off. I want to try for the prize money, and while I know that's unrealistic because, let's face it, Theo is an unmitigated disaster with a machine, I can try. And hopefully that translates to outside of the show success, which will then feed into money I can save to buy into Bloom."

Annie wiped her hands with a napkin. "If you need a loan, I can help."

I forced a smile. "I know. I want to try and do this myself first."

"I respect that."

"We're here if you need us," Frankie said, brushing stray pink strands from her face. "Seriously. Call any time."

Tears of thankfulness burned at the back of my eyes, but I forced them away. "I know. I love you guys."

"Nawww." Flo flopped onto me, wrapping me in a hug. "We love you too, little stitch."

I chuckled. "Okay, enough mushiness. Let's talk books."

"Oh my God." Annie shot upright, startling Ace who had been dozing by Flo's feet. The dog's ears twitched before he settled back down to resume his sleep. "Did you guys get to chapter eighteen? I swear I had to call Linc to come home and help me out after reading that scene." Annie fanned herself. "Phew! That author should take out shares in vibrators."

Chuckling, I let the conversation soothe the rough edges that today's events had chipped into my calm, grateful for my friends and their support.

What will be will be, I reminded myself. Tomorrow would be here soon enough.

CHAPTER 6
THEO

MAI

I think I want to climb a mountain

THEO

You hate physical exercise

MAI

Says who?

THEO

You. You literally complained the entire time
I took you hiking

MAI

Your version of hiking involved snakes,
wolves and a snowstorm. I feel my protests
were justified

THEO

It wasn't that bad

MAI

Tell that to the rangers who had to carry
you out...

THEO

And here I was thinking you liked adventure

Airport security always took forever when I traveled. They'd spend extra time doing pat downs and chemical testing to make sure I wasn't smuggling drugs or ammunition in through my prosthetic.

"And arms," the bored security guard said, gesturing for me to lift them.

"Don't worry, the only thing I'm packing is a shit-ton of cheese in my bag," I told him with a wink.

The guard ignored me, completing his examination.

Guess he didn't enjoy my cheese jokes.

With a few swipes of some pads, he checked for chemical residue, then dismissed me.

"Next," he called, turning away.

Free to go, I picked up my bag and made my way to where Mai stood, fiddling anxiously as she glanced around the airport.

"All done?" she asked.

I nodded, watching as she tapped the fingertips of one hand against the ring I'd given her. The Morse-code-like movement had become a tell for her stress levels.

I caught her hand, gently squeezing until her fingers relaxed.

"We're down here," I said, leading her toward the terminal. "But you already knew that."

Her cheeks flushed and she dipped her head, hiding her

face behind her curtain of ebony hair. "I may have glanced at the board."

Mai never left anything to chance. She did better with certainties, working through her anxiety by understanding how things were laid out, what was expected of her, how she should dress or behave. Her overpreparation had saved my bacon a time or two, but I knew it cost her mentally and physically.

Following an uneventful plane ride, we were met at the airport by a smiling, peppy young man with the unexpected name of Bruce. Bruces in my opinion were men who sprouted from the earth at the age of forty, with peppered beards, pot bellies and who only drank beer that came in cans.

This Bruce seemed determined to shake my belief in the name to the core. He appeared to be no older than twenty-one, had lime-green hair with a single flop of ice white at his left temple that contrasted sharply with his fake tan. He wore the shit out of a crisp flowing dress that looked like it came from a scene in *The Devil Wears Prada*.

I glanced down at my own simple plaid button-up and jeans. *We're not in Kansas anymore, Toto.*

Mai clutched my hand as we followed him.

"This way!" Bruce said, quickly navigating the crowds of the airport. "We'll need to hurry if we're going to make it on time. The other couples all landed yesterday, but there was an issue booking your tickets so late—that's what happens when you're a last-minute addition."

Mai stumbled and I caught her, holding her close.

"An addition?" she repeated.

"Yeah." Bruce nodded. "The other couple broke up.

Completely understandable—they were nightmares throughout this whole casting process. We were desperate and you two seemed like the best option to replace them at short notice."

He held the door open for us and we stepped into the midafternoon sun.

"Why do you say that?" I asked.

"You're from a small town, determined to make it big. You're unknowns on the fashion circuit, and while your design samples were good...." He made a gesture with his hands that I took to mean he wasn't overly impressed with Mai's efforts.

I bristled. "Are you saying that—"

"Here it is," Bruce interrupted, ignoring me.

A black limo slid into the pickup space, idling by the curb.

"Theo."

I glanced down at Mai, my jaw clenched. She smiled up at me, her expression serene.

"It's okay," she assured me, squeezing my hand. "We knew coming in we were the underdogs. It's not a problem."

I blew out a breath. "You're right." I forced a smile. "Should we make underdog t-shirts to wear on our first day? Perhaps a hound dog expression with 'Underdogs are the best dogs' written above it."

Mai snorted. "We'd be tossed out."

"You say that, and yet I've seen some of the things celebrities wear." I helped her slide into the back of the limo. "Our shirt would be iconic."

"I doubt that very much."

Bruce followed me in then shut the door, sealing us into the dim interior.

I'd never traveled in a limo before and was surprised to find it... underwhelming. Oh, sure there were snacks, interesting lighting, and a cool partition that separated us from the driver, but otherwise, it was just a car. And cars didn't hold any appeal for me.

The woman seated beside me, dressed in a cute sundress of her own making, however...

"Theo!"

I pulled my hand back from the control panel, flashing Mai a sheepish grin. "What?"

She inclined her head toward the driver. "I'm sure they don't enjoy you opening and closing the partition repeatedly."

I muttered something petulant under my breath but leaned back in my seat.

Bruce laughed, holding up his phone. "You mind scooting closer together? I want to snap a picture of you two for our socials."

We exchanged a glance but did as asked. Bruce twisted this way and that, taking picture after picture, directing us to "look natural" and "smile more."

How one smiled with all their teeth while looking natural I would never know.

A tinge of exhaustion hit me as the limo pulled into the hotel driveway. My residual limb had begun to throb on the plane—no doubt a mixture of swelling from the pressure and from all the walking on slippery surfaces—tiles were the bane of my existence.

"I'm looking forward to room service and bed," I admitted quietly to Mai as we shuffled to exit the limo.

"Oh, did I not mention tonight's events?" Bruce asked, overhearing our conversation.

"Mention what?" I asked, straightening from the car.

"We have interviews scheduled followed by welcome drinks. You'll meet the host and the other teams. It's compulsory."

Mai and I exchanged a frustrated look.

"No," I said tightly. "It must have slipped your mind while you were taking a million pictures of our shoes."

He chuckled, seemingly oblivious to my sarcasm. "Don't worry, makeup is on standby and will have you looking incredible before you can even blink."

"Will there be food?" Mai asked, patting her stomach. "I don't think I'll be able to form a sentence if I'm not fed."

Bruce pulled out his phone, swiping rapidly. "The schedule doesn't mention eating, but I'll see that something is delivered. Though" —he sniffed delicately— "you really should have eaten on the plane."

"How silly of us," I drawled, clutching a hand to my chest. "We shall make a note to do so next time."

Mai elbowed me in the side, a not-so-subtle hint.

I glanced down at her, our gazes meeting in a silent conversation.

Play nice.

I frowned, tipping my head toward Bruce.

I don't want to. The guy is an ass.

She sighed, her expression turning pleading.

Please?

Rolling my eyes, I dropped an arm over her shoulder and pulled her into my side.

"Only for you," I murmured against her ear. "But if there's no food in the next fifteen minutes, all bets are off."

Our bags were handed off to a doorman before Bruce ushered us through the doors of the beautiful hotel, through another set of doors, and into a conference room that had been repurposed into a studio. The second our feet crossed the threshold a whirlwind of activity engulfed us.

"Smile," an audio tech barked at me as she ripped my shirt from my body and began to strap a microphone to my chest. "You're about to be a star."

Microphone strapped down, my shirt was quickly replaced by a different woman who ushered us forward. Tall and lean, she had the kind of mannerisms that reminded me of a person who'd had three cups too many coffee. We followed, listening as she pointed out different areas of the staging. While she moved confidently through the chaos, Mai and I struggled, dodging bustling crew who were more focused on their miles of cables than the fresh meat walking by.

"I'm the director. You're on my set," the woman said, flicking dark-brown hair away from her tired face. "Which means I own you. When I say jump, you don't ask how high, you just jump. Got me?"

I bristled, glancing at Mai. Her expression had blanked, but I read panic in her eyes. That panic was enough to calm whatever annoyance I felt. I was here for her—not me. I needed to check my ego at the door and just go with the flow.

We nodded, Mai's hand finding mine as we walked.

"Good. We're going to do couple interviews. You sit on a couch, you answer all the questions, and then you get to go join the other contestants at the party. Got me?"

I shot Mai a teasing look. "Aye, aye, Captain."

The imposing woman glanced at me over her shoulder, her gaze narrowing. "A joker, are you? We'll see how much you're laughing once the competition starts."

I exchanged a look with Mai, feeling strangely like a scolded schoolboy.

"She doesn't like you," Mai whispered, barely containing her laughter. "We're already off to a horrible start."

"No one hates me," I said confidently. "They just don't know they like me yet."

"Sit. It's time to prove you can charm the public." The director clapped her hands like we were schoolkids and not grown-ass adults.

"What's your name?" I asked, as we sat.

"Celeste, but you can call me sir."

I swallowed a laugh. "Yes, sir."

From seemingly nowhere, makeup artists appeared, plastering my face with creams and dust and something they called setting spray before scurrying off to leave us alone with the host of the show—Michelle Conliam.

Once named one of the most beautiful women in the world, the former model hadn't lost an ounce of her charisma since her retirement. Her brown skin gleamed under the studio lights, and despite now being in her mid-forties, her close-cropped black hair showed only the faintest of gray in the strands.

She wore a dress that put me in mind of dancing—a red

flirty number that clung to her frame and showed off her sinuous, lean limbs.

"Welcome," she said warmly, clasping first Mai's hands, then mine. "I'm so pleased to meet you both. Are you excited to be here?"

Mai nodded mutely, forcing me to step in.

"Thrilled," I said, covering for her. "But a little shell-shocked, if I'm honest. Ain't every day you're flown halfway across the country and dropped into a set like this."

Michelle chuckled. "Don't worry, we'll look after you."

"And, three, two, one, action!" a man with a clapboard yelled, smacking the board before stepping out of view.

Under the glaring lights of the interview set, I could feel every ounce of makeup caked on my face as the host fired questions about our "relationship."

I shot Mai a quick glance, registering her frozen expression and the vacant look in her eyes.

Fuck.

Her hands were clasped in her lap, but I could see her fingers tap-tap-tapping up and down the back of her hand.

Come on, Mai. You can do it.

When she didn't speak, I decided to intervene. Casually, I shifted across the couch until I could press my side against hers. Wrapping one arm over her shoulders, I took her hands in mine and settled them on my lap.

She glanced up at me, but I ignored her, staring at Michelle.

"What do you like best about Mai?" Michelle asked, her expression amused.

"What's not to like?" I responded lightly. "She's an incredible human. She's the kind of person who sees a family on an outing and offers to take a photo of all of them because she doesn't want anyone to miss out on being in the memory."

Mai stiffened beside me, her head tilting back as she stared up at me.

"When we go out, it'll always take us twice as long to get to where we're going because she can't just walk from A to B. She wants to take the longer route—moving this way and that to capture all the things that life offers."

I huffed out a laugh. "The first time we went on a hike she brought a plastic bag with her to collect rubbish. She never made a big deal about it, but I noticed because that's the kind of person she is—kind and generous and someone who cares about the small stuff. The people in her life know we matter to her because she lets us know every day how she feels in a million different ways."

I glanced down at her, seeing her wide eyes.

"What?" I asked defensively. "It's true."

"I never... I didn't know you thought that."

I brushed the back of my knuckles against her cheek. "You're an easy person to love."

As a friend... right? my inner voice wanted to know.

Michelle gently broke the tension simmering between us.

"And you, Mai? What do you like best about Theo?"

Mai's gaze stayed locked with mine.

"Everything." The corners of her lips lifted, her gaze warming. "Theo's like a rainbow after the rain. No matter how bleak the day may have been, no matter how hopeless the situation seems, he appears, and you just know everything is going to work out. Not because it's better, but because he makes it easier to bear. He stands beside you, encouraging you, supporting you, being this practical but funny guy. He makes you believe you can conquer the world."

My chest tightened, and I found myself swallowing a lump that had formed in my throat.

This isn't real. It's all make-believe.

"Is that why you entered this competition?" Michelle asked.

Slowly, seemingly reluctantly, Mai pulled her gaze away from me to answer Michelle. "I didn't actually enter," she admitted. "Theo did it for me. I'd have never had the courage."

Michelle sighed dreamily. "What a wonderful relationship. Now, let's move on to something fun. Favorite thing to do together?"

"Easy," I replied. "Eat late-night ramen and binge old sitcoms."

"Your design style?"

Mai lifted her hands, finally relaxing enough to become lost in the conversation. "I'm passionate about sustainability. My designs are all about wearability. I want people to be able to take something and wear it time and time again, and for it to continue to feel new and different each time."

"I love that," Michelle said, clapping her hands. "I can't wait to see what you bring to this competition."

After what felt like an eternity of probing, we were finally released into the wild—also known as the mixer.

Exhausted—and me with a headache building—we walked into the room to find the event in full swing. The studio had chosen this hotel as it had a giant convention space attached. It was in the convention warehouse that they'd created a decadent fashion show space, complete with a stage and runway.

I glanced around, trying to figure out if this is where we'd be filming or if they had another, separate space set up.

Music pumped over the loudspeakers, while the crowd shuffled and flowed, bumping against us. The lights in the room were dim with spotlights highlighting models who stood on small platforms around the room.

"They're wearing designs by the judges," Mai said, hushed reverence in her voice. "That one is worth millions of dollars—I think one of the royal family wore it."

I glanced at the dress but was more interested in finding some chow. "Do you think there's food here?

Mai raised up on tiptoe, trying to peek over the top of the crowd. "I can't see anything."

I sighed heavily. "Guess we better wander around and see what we can scavenge. I'm not above cannibalism at this point."

Mai linked her arm with mine. "Chin up, we can hit room service soon."

Gorgeous people in gorgeous clothing stood everywhere, chatting and laughing as they sipped wine and admired the models. In my ear, Mai kept up a running commentary of who was who, regularly gasping and fangirling over different designers and models as they moved around us.

I knew she was talented; it's why I'd wanted her to be on this show. But seeing her here, in this room, surrounded by people she followed and designers she admired, I discovered a new side to Mai I hadn't known existed.

She belongs.

"Jesus," I murmured to Mai as we passed yet another cluster of people dressed in every shade of black. "Are we at a fashion show or a funeral?"

She snorted, leaning into my side. "Charcoal and taupe are very popular this season."

I looked pointedly at her pastel blue dress.

"I know," she laughed. "I prefer color. It's very last season."

I glanced down at the outfit she'd made me. While I'd been working around the clock to master the basics, Mai had laid down some serious thread to craft me a wardrobe for the competition.

"I need to represent myself," she'd explained, crouching between my legs as she'd pinned my inseam. "Which means you need to be wearing designs by me."

"I'd wear a napkin if you made it," I'd said loyally.

"Let's hope I can pull together something a little more concealing. No one wants to see your ass on TV."

"Not when you can see it in real life, right?" I'd asked with a grin, flexing my ass cheeks.

She'd blushed and made me pay for my teasing by forcing me to try and create a three-piece suit. Torture.

We made our way around the room, finally finding a waiter offering canapes and some decidedly non-alcoholic drinks.

"You must be the last couple," a warm voice said, interrupting Mai's explanation of the beauty of one of the outfits on display. "I'm Gretchen Mishra, and this is my partner, Jodie."

We turned to find a middle-aged couple standing behind us. They wore matching outfits of sparkling leather pants, and fringed vests. It was like Dolly Parton had designed it.

"I'm Mai and this is Theo," Mai said, introducing us. "We're excited to be here."

We chatted for a bit, Mai asking about their designs and background while I listened politely. The pair were from Chars. They'd met at design school, and fused Gretchen's Pakistani heritage with Jodie's passion for grunge and country, opening an urban street wear brand that specialized in servicing actors and music artists.

"We better keep circulating," Jodie said reluctantly, glancing over Mai's shoulder. "I'd love to stay but you're about to be interrogated by the ice twins."

"Ice?" I asked, turning to follow their gaze. "What do you mean?"

Gretchen and Jodie faded away as another couple approached. They wore matching tight-fitting suits and looked more like a brother and sister ready for a red-carpet affair rather than this casual party.

"Jude," the taller of the two said, presenting his hand to me. "And you are?"

I felt Mai shrink beside me, crowding closer. I'd begun to relax, thinking this seemed like a nice place—apart from the overly stressed director. Seeing the way the guy looked down his nose at us, I could see my assumption may have been premature.

I took his hand, shaking it firmly. "Theo and Mai, pleased to meet you."

"Quite," Jude said, eyeing Mai. "I know you from somewhere. Tell me how."

She hesitated, a flush dusting her cheeks. "I took your course three years ago."

Jude's gaze narrowed on Mai. "You cried."

Mai hunched her shoulders, nodding.

He tutted under his breath.

Unimpressed, I wrapped an arm around Mai, hauling her into my side.

"And which houses have you interned?" Keeley asked, sniffing delicately.

The two of them gave me strong villain vibes, and I did not like that for us.

"Mai's house," I said easily. "She's a great teacher."

Mai spluttered as Keeley and Jude stared at me as if I'd lost my mind.

"They mean fashion houses," Mai corrected gently. "But Theo's correct. He's only ever worked with me."

As if they'd practiced it, the two evildoers exchanged a glance and as one, dismissed us as competition.

Keeley's gaze dropped to my prosthetic. "Are you the sob story, hired to pull the ratings?"

I chuckled at their obvious attempts to intimidate me—the one guy who had zero skin in this game—but Mai didn't seem to be on the same page. She bristled, stepping in front of me.

"That was rude," she informed her, her expression fierce. "Theo and I are here to win this."

"Best of luck with that," Jude said with an insincere

smirk. "I don't think you'll be able to cry yourself to victory."

Hot rage burned through me like wildfire, but I bit my tongue, determined to take the high road with these two wankers.

"Good luck," I responded sweetly, taking hold of Mai before she began to scratch their eyes out. "Buh-bye now."

She allowed me to drag her away but not before loudly voicing her protest.

"I could have taken them," she spat, glaring over her shoulder.

"I know, babe. But they're not worth it. They'll learn how wrong they are when you win this thing."

Mai straightened her dress, flicking agitatedly at her skirts. "We don't have to win, we just have to beat them."

"Noted. Now, what's this about crying and a course?"

"Oh man," Mai crumbled. "It's so embarrassing. Yasmin and Maeve sent me to a course a few years ago. Keeley is one of the world's best corset designers. Everything was going well until the end of the week when I started getting anxious about the judging—we had to present in front of a room and I despise public speaking. I freaked myself out and burst into tears just as I finished presenting."

She shook her head, her cheeks flushed with embarrassment.

"I take it the Douche Canoes weren't exactly sympathetic."

"Jude asked me to leave."

I winced. "Ouch."

She sighed heavily. "I did a really good job too."

"Changing topic, how soon before we can blow this popsicle joint?" I asked, ready to find a bed.

"Surely soon. They know we've been up since dawn. They can't expect us to hang around much longer."

But alas, our prayers were not to be answered.

"Contestants, can you approach the stage please?"

We exchanged a glance as we walked up, taking our position as directed.

"And 3, 2—" The director pointed at the stage.

Music began to pump over the loud system as the lights dimmed. On the far side of the room sat a stage, from which Michelle walked out, a spotlight following her catwalk. She'd changed in the hour since we'd left her side, and now wore a ball gown fit for the red carpet.

My stomach sank like a stone when I spotted camera crews making their way toward the competing couples.

Shit.

If this went how I anticipated, we weren't getting to bed any time soon.

My stomach grumbled loudly, issuing a protest.

"Welcome, competitors!" Michelle called, striking a pose. "Are you ready to take the fashion world by storm?"

Around us, the crowd cheered while Mai and I stood quietly.

"This year, six fashion-forward couples are fighting to create fabulous looks that will leave us breathless." Michelle threw her arms out to the audience, and a spotlight hit us, blinding me.

Fuck!

"This is the moment when thread and fabric weave together to create a dream. But will you succeed, or will the pressure of the competition unravel all you've worked so hard to achieve?"

I leaned over to whisper in Mai's ear. "This is some of the corniest shit I've ever heard."

"Shh," she hushed. "We need to focus."

Michelle explained the terms of the show and how the lowest performing couples would be eliminated until a champion could be crowned. The dollar figures danced a cancan in my head, while an image of Mai's ecstatic face swam before me.

I'm gonna do everything in my power to help her to win.

"Your first challenge is to create a fabulous feminine red-carpet look." Michelle dipped, showing off her dress. "This is a non-elimination round, but while the pressure might be off, I'm about to turn the heat up."

She spun, holding out a hand to the back of the stage. An older man dressed in a bright-pink jumpsuit stepped onto the stage, his shock of white hair and almost-translucent skin contrasted with his bright orange glasses.

"Oh my God," Mai breathed, her face a picture of stunned awe. "It's Erike Baretti."

"A man who needs no introductions," Michelle said with a laugh. "Erike Baretti!"

I applauded politely, having no clue who the hell this guy was and why my fake girlfriend might be in raptures over him.

"Welcome, designers," he said, his voice soft but stern. "There will be two prizes handed out tomorrow—the first will be to the team our judges deem to have constructed the best outfit. And the second, will be revealed following the event."

He bowed his head. "Teams, you have just eight hours to create your finished design." A giant clock appeared on the wall behind him, the projection reading eight hours.

"Your time starts... now!"

I blanched as the crowd scattered and the other couples took off running.

"I'm sorry," I said, staring at Mai who stared back at me. "Did he say, *now*?"

She nodded, her mouth opening and closing.

"Fuck." I glanced around. "Surely they're joking. We've been up since four this morning. We need food and sleep. You're dead on your feet and I'm—"

"Run!" Celeste barked, throwing her clipboard at me. "Get going!"

"Jesus!" I narrowly avoided the flying plastic. "Fine! We're going!" I grabbed Mai's hand and tugged her along. "I think this is a hostile work environment."

She snorted. "Welcome to fashion, darling."

CHAPTER 7
MAI

THEO

You ever feel like a waste of space?

MAI

No

THEO

Oh good, me either

MAI

What happened?

THEO

Nothing

MAI

Why don't I believe you?

THEO

On an unrelated note, how do you feel about me becoming a monk? Good, bad, indifferent?

MAI

So the date didn't go well?

THEO

They went to the bathroom and never returned

MAI

I'm on my way

My heart pounded against my rib cage as the reality of our situation hit me like a ton of bricks.

Around us, the crowd moved back as the other couples tossed their food and drink and sprinted toward the fabric room, claiming material and patterns in a dog-eat-dog fight.

"Ready?" Theo asked, dropping my hand to present his arm to me.

I blinked up at him, my mind racing a million miles an hour. "Eight hours. We only have eight hours."

He brushed his knuckles over my cheek. "And we're going to get it done in seven hours and fifty-eight minutes."

A hysterical bubble of laughter clawed up my throat. "There's no way."

"There's always a way." He began to guide me toward a spare workstation. "Think, Mai. What is going to be the quickest and easiest style to achieve in the time we have while still looking fabulous?"

A hundred scenarios and options flicked through my mind as I settled at the table and reached for a sketch pad.

"You draw," Theo said, plonking hands on my shoulders. "I'm gonna go claim some fabric before these vultures pick it clean."

"Satin and velvet," I instructed, an idea beginning to

take shape. "In two colors—like a muted or primary color and something exciting."

"Black and pink?" he asked.

"That would work, but make the pink bold. Black and pastels have been done before."

He nodded as I became aware of a camera crew moving our way. I glanced at them, then bent my head to the paper, starting to sketch out a rough idea. "Hurry, Theo."

"I'm on it."

The design had to be simple to pull together in the time we had. Something elegant, sophisticated, and timeless, but daring and bold in execution.

Not an easy feat.

I tore up the first design, tossing the paper in the trash. Cold sweat trickled down my back as I clutched at my pens, staring at the fresh, white sheet.

Yasmin had once said a blank page was a most fearsome thing, and up until this moment, I hadn't understood what she meant. Now I did. Staring at the sketch pad, my mind raced so quickly everything jumbled until it became a blur of nothingness.

Michelle made her way over to me, an envelope in her hands.

"You'll need this," she said, handing me the gold paper.

Trying hard not to have a breakdown in the first ten minutes of the show, I slid the blade of my scissors under the lip and withdrew three papers, each with different measurements.

Another twist," she said with a grin. "You have three models to choose from. Good luck."

I quickly scanned the pages. Two were similar sizing to

traditional models, tall with lean proportions, while the third posed a more interesting challenge.

When people thought of the fashion industry, they often imagined famous models like Miranda Kerr or Tyra Banks or Kendall Jenner. These were models that had to be a certain size and shape to meet the high fashion requirements for garments. These cream-of-the-crop runway models were hired to fit the clothes the designers made—rather than the designers creating the clothes to fit them. Usually tall with precise waist, bust, and hip measurements, they were hired for those proportions.

However, a newer trend had emerged over the previous decade, one which I wholeheartedly endorsed. These were high-end runway models who bucked traditional standards, women like Ashley Graham, Precious Lee, and Paloma Elsesser, who were mid-sized or larger, shorter or taller, and due to their unusual proportions, designers created clothes to complement their body and embrace their uniqueness rather than using the model as a living coat hanger.

I plucked the last measurements from the small pile, turning to the adjustable mannequin as a dress began to take shape in my mind.

An off-the-shoulder with a sweetheart peek-a-boo neckline and fitted A-line skirt. We'd draw attention to her waist and breasts to create a gorgeous silhouette. We'd add drama with a beautiful double-sided train that attached to her hand with a gorgeous silver chain.

I sucked in a deep breath, feeling as if I could breathe for the first time since our plane had landed.

"Here we go." Theo dumped rolls and rolls of fabric

onto our workbench, attempting to catch them as they rolled this way and that.

A black velvet caught my eye, along with a stunningly vibrant fuchsia satin.

"These two," I said, discarding the rest. "If I draw the patterns, can you cut?"

"I think I can do that."

We exchanged a wry grin.

"Remember what I taught you about cutting velvet?" I asked as I reached for my sketch pad.

Theo lifted one hand to his chin, cupping his jaw. "Something about the pattern and fluffing."

"Shedding," I corrected as I began to sketch out the design. "We need to plan how to cut this carefully—and we don't use pins, we use weights. Velvet's too delicate."

"Gotcha." He reached for a pair of scissors. "Just tell me what you want, and I'll do it."

I finished the quick sketch and held it up for him to see. "Thoughts?"

"I like it. It'll be awesome."

I heard a murmur behind us, the last few words of the conversation reaching my ears.

"...check if he can sew?"

My shoulders tensed, the hair on the back of my neck prickling.

Oh, God. We're going to be found out. We'll be ostracized. I'll never be able to work in—

"But will it have pockets?"

A shock of laughter burst out of me at Theo's unexpected question. "What?"

"Pockets. For snacks. I assume red carpet means a long-ass event. People are bound to get hungry." He tapped his stomach. "I know I could eat."

There was a snort from the camera crew, and I began to relax, the pressure easing a little.

"We'll see if we have time."

He gestured at the long train. "Be cool if that was hollow or had a zip. You could fill it with chips and chocolate."

"Theo!"

"What?" he asked, shooting me a grin. "You're saying you wouldn't want a sneaky snack mid-performance? Imagine wearing this thing to the cinema. You could smuggle a whole minibar in."

I rolled my eyes but noted gratefully that the film crew appeared to be amused rather than suspicious.

I pushed the bolt of satin toward him. "Just roll this out."

I measured out the pattern pieces on large sheets of paper then handed them to Theo to cut down to size. Once we had all the parts laid out and pinned or weighted on the fabric, we began to cut the pieces we'd need.

Around us, machines whirred, and teams called instructions to one another as they worked rapidly to cut, pin, press, and sew each part of their design.

Pressure slowly built upon my shoulders, like sand trickling to settle at the bottom of an hourglass—each second adding one more grain of pressure.

It doesn't matter if you win or lose. It's a non-elimination round. You just need to get through today.

Our workbench became a makeshift battlefield, scissors and pins our weapons of choice. With pattern pieces now complete, I pinned while Theo pressed. We worked in unison, passing the pieces back and forth like a conveyor line.

"Four hours left," Michelle called from the stage. "Tools down for the moment, please. We'll take a ten-minute mandatory break, then get back into it."

"Shit," Theo grunted, standing from his seat. "My back is killing me."

I noted he didn't speak about his leg, but judging by how he leaned, I guessed it also pained him.

"Are you okay? Do you need me to track down some painkillers?"

Theo waved me off. "I'm fine. I just need coffee and to stretch."

My foot jiggled nervously as I glanced around at the other teams. They were far more advanced than us—many having already completed various pieces of their outfit.

"Damn," Theo said, tilting his head to one side as he surveyed the competition. "Are we slow or are they fast?"

"Both?" Unable to remain seated, I stood, stretching out my shoulders and neck as water bottles, cups of coffee, and snacks were handed out. "We're really behind."

Theo shrugged. "We'll make it up. I have faith."

"I'm glad you do," I muttered, rubbing my temples. "I'm not sure I can pull together something of this magnitude in four hours."

"Hey, look at me." Theo's hands were warm and comforting on my shoulders as he turned me toward him. "What have we got left to do?"

"Finish the pinning, actually sew or hand stitch the pieces, and then assemble."

"So three things. Easy."

I snorted. "Not quite three but I appreciate the sentiment."

His hands pressed into my shoulders, massaging the stress from my aching muscles. I groaned, closing my eyes as his thumbs glided over my shoulders and up my neck, the slow sweep hypnotizing as he dissipated the tension from my body.

"We can do this, Mai. I have faith."

"I should be doing this to you," I said, tilting my head to give him better access.

He chuckled, his warm breath dancing across the shell of my ear. "Later."

We broke apart to eat a small serving of fruit and yoghurt, then settled back at our bench as the director began a countdown.

"In three, two, one." Celeste pointed at Michelle.

"Four hours left!" she called once more. "Better kick those machines into top gear because the end is near!"

The remainder of our pieces were quickly assembled, and then Theo and I sat down to begin the process of assembling the dress. I gave him the easy pieces—the ones which didn't require perfectly straight lines.

Together we whizzed through the construction of the pieces, and I found myself surprised by Theo's dedication to precision.

"How's this?" he asked, handing me one of the panels that would form the train.

I examined the stitching, noting a few missteps but nothing that would require a complete redo.

"Great." I glanced up, smiling at him. "You're really improving."

"Improving? That doesn't bode well for your team, Ms. Sakamoto."

I stiffened, turning slowly to see that Michelle and Erike had approached our workstation while our backs were turned.

Oh, crap.

Just when I thought I had a handle on my panic, a new test arrived to send me spiraling once more.

I never realized I was a masochist.

Theo covered for me, easily sliding into the awkwardness.

"Gonna be honest," he said with an "aw shucks" smile. "Mai's the brains, talent and beauty behind this operation. I'm barely trained in the basics. But we're here, we're enthusiastic, and I'm open to learning."

Michelle and Erike exchanged a loaded glance.

"What do you mean by 'barely trained'?" Erike asked, crossing his arms.

My mouth opened to try and cover for Theo, but he beat me to the punch.

"Just that. Mai's been teaching me for the last year, but progress is slow. But isn't that the point of this show? To profile couples just trying to pursue a dream?"

Erike cocked an eyebrow as Michelle rushed to reassure us.

"Absolutely! All of our couples are in different stages of their fashion journey, and we welcome everyone—from beginner to master."

"Don't you feel guilty for depriving a more worthy pair of their dream?" Erike interrupted.

I swallowed, horrified that I may have disappointed my hero.

Theo stared him down, shifting to block me slightly. "No. Mai's dream is valid, and she deserves this chance just as much as anyone else—more even. I might slow her down but I'm not here to hold her back."

I stared up at Theo, watching as a muscle ticked in his jaw. His fierce protectiveness left me feeling warm and fuzzy.

"And on that note," Michelle said hastily, "we should leave you both to finish." She turned to the room at large. "Two hours left!"

The clock became our merciless overlord, a villain in our story. We finished the machine work and switched to hand stitching as the time counted down.

Theo and I worked well together, communicating openly and honestly when something wasn't working. He surprised me with suggestions to problems I would never have even contemplated. We were becoming a well-oiled machine, even if one half of the machine was still learning which part was the bobbin and which was the feed dog.

"Your models have arrived," Michelle called as women streamed into the design area.

As I'd predicted, the majority of the teams had chosen to build a dress that the model would need to fit, but for us—and one other team—we'd elected to design the dress for the model.

"Keeley and Jude," Theo told me with a conspiratorial air. "I got the lowdown from one of the show runners.

They're tipped to take out the entire competition but we're gonna give them a run for their money."

While I appreciated his enthusiasm, I didn't have time for small talk.

"Can you find a small silver chain?" I asked, showing him where I wanted it sewn. "It's the last piece on the train. I need to finish the bodice."

"On it."

Our model arrived, a gorgeous woman whose proportions reminded me of Kate Winslet or Beatrix Bellinger.

"Wow," she said, eyeing the dress. "This is incredible."

I took a moment to critically eye our creation as a whole rather than the individual parts that still needed attention. She wasn't wrong. The dress had flair and drama, with the bold fabric choices creating an edgy vibe that still presented as classical elegance thanks to the simple silhouette.

"I'm Sophia, by the way."

I held out my hand. "Mai. Are you ready to try it on?"

She nodded enthusiastically. "Let's do it."

The dress fit her like a glove, creating sensual, feminine lines. There were a few small tweaks required to ensure the bodice lay flat, but as I finished, I glanced at the time, laughing when I saw that Theo hadn't been too far off his prediction.

"Seven hours and fifty-three minutes," I teased him, as he fiddled with the chain hanging from Sophia's wrist. "Turns out we beat the—"

In startling slow motion, I saw Theo step back and onto a scrap of fabric, his prosthetic rolling forward. His gaze met mine as he slipped backward, arms flailing. I reached out, trying to grab him but it was too late. He fell, his legs kicking up.

Like something out of a horror movie, his boot caught on the train of the dress, and as it dropped, it pulled the fabric, ripping the chain free and leaving a large gaping tear in the beautiful fabric.

Around us, all movement ceased as people stared in silent horror. Then the camera crew rushed in as the world kicked back into gear.

"Shit!" Theo cursed, struggling to untangle himself from the mess. "Fuck and shit!"

I dropped to my knees, frantically searching his body for injury.

"Are you hurt? Shit, are you—"

He waved me off. "Forget about me. Go! Do what you can to salvage my fucking mistake."

"But—"

He gave me a little push. "Go, Mai. Hurry!"

I glanced at the clock, my heart pounding in my throat. Six minutes.

"Sophia, go to the machine," I ordered. "Theo, I—"

"Just go!"

Shit!

I didn't have any time to argue with him. With Sophia still wearing the gown, I collected my wits, knowing I'd have to sew the ripped fabric without pins or measurements, and pray I didn't make a dog's breakfast of it.

"Get on the table," I ordered Sophia as I gathered the fabric. "We need to make sure the weight of the dress doesn't pull at the hem or it's going to be an even bigger disaster."

She did as directed without protest, climbing up and shifting until I could feed the fabric through the machine.

My fingers worked overtime as I tucked and sewed, creating a hem that, while not exactly straight or tidy, remained functional and hid the worst of the damage.

"One minute!"

"Please, please, please, please, please," I chanted as I fed the machine as quickly as I could without causing it to jam. "Come on, come on, come on."

I cut the thread with thirty seconds to spare, tugging the black elastic from my hair, I quickly handstitched it into the dress, closing the seam. I wouldn't have time to replace the chain so this would have to do.

"Tools down!"

Stepping back, I held my hands up, breathing heavily as I glanced frantically over the dress.

It wasn't perfect but it would do.

Non-elimination, I reminded myself as I struggled to catch my breath. *The only stakes on the table are the ones you've built in your head.*

Sophia grinned at me as the camera crew swirled around us, catching each chest-rattling breath I fought to suck in.

"You did it." She threaded her middle finger through the elastic, wrapping it around her finger twice. "Not as pretty as the chain but it works."

She moved her hand back and forth, the train following her movements.

An avalanche of emotion hit me, crushing the breath from my lungs.

"I have to, I mean, I—"

"Go see your partner." Sophia nodded, smiling. "I'll see you after the show."

I pushed through the crowds of people milling about as crew raced here and there, setting up for the runway event.

"Mai!"

I spun, spotting Theo sitting on a chair beside a woman in green scrubs.

"Theo." Relief hit, and for a second, I swayed on my feet as the world tilted.

"Whoa!" Theo caught me, pulling me into his arms. "Take a load off before you collapse."

"I'm okay," I said, shaking my head a little to clear it. "I'm just—"

"Exhausted, starving, overwhelmed?" Theo asked, glaring at Bruce as he walked toward us.

We ignored him. "How are you? What do you need?"

"Nothing, I'll be fine."

"Rest," the medic interrupted. "He's got some bruising but should be okay."

Bruce intruded on our little group, placing his hands on his hips. "The show is about to resume. If you're both cleared by the medic, follow me."

The medic nodded and so off we went, following him like little ducks through the chaos and into the interview room. The runway was projected onto a giant screen along one wall, while an array of comfortable seating had been positioned across the floor in front of the screen.

"Looks like we're the last," Theo murmured, guiding me across to the only set of empty seats left in the back corner.

Once seated, I took the opportunity to consider our competition. Some were designers whose work I admired, like Nina and Dakila Basa. They had established their street wear brand three years ago, and everyone from Wolf Rodriguez to Justice Wild wore their designs.

In addition to Nina and Dakila, there were Meg and Bec Pecherczyk, Alec and Tempest De Soto, Gretchen and Jodie, and, of course, Keeley Walters and Jude O'Malley.

I had wondered how the show might portray me as a woman of color. If there'd be endless questions about my heritage, whether my parents approved of my choices, if they'd write me off because I was an introverted, Japanese woman. But seeing my competitors and the hosts, and knowing they represented the Black, Filipino, Chilean, and First Nations communities gave me a sense of comfort.

Perhaps this wouldn't be as burdensome as I'd assumed.

Music began to play from the speakers around the room, and the lights dimmed as the runway projection lit up the screen.

"Here we go," Theo murmured.

Music pumped loudly as the first model strutted out. She wore Nina and Dakila's design, an oversized puffer jacket dress made from latex and covered in hand-painted graffiti. It swamped the model, whose only visible body part happened to be her head.

"Grunge meets red carpet," Erike said, the camera panning to where he sat in the audience. "An interesting choice."

On one side of him sat Michelle, on the other sat Minerva Devillian, the editor of *Vogue Astipia*, and Alison Louis, a former model turned fashion director to the stars. If she liked a design and put one of her clients in it, you were guaranteed to be a knockout success.

"I don't know," Alison said, tapping an elegant finger against her jaw. "An artist attending the Oscars does so to be seen. This would work better as a dress for the Royal Gala, rather than an awards night."

"I agree," Minerva nodded. "There's no finesse. The execution is excellent but how does one capture this on film? How does it portray the beauty and grace of the wearer?"

"We're agreed," Erike declared. "It's a disastrous choice for the challenge—no matter how much we might like it."

I glanced at where the Basas sat and winced at their devastated expressions.

"Ouch," Theo said. "Brutal."

"They are judges."

"True. But a little 'finesse,'"—he made finger quotes with his hands—"wouldn't go astray."

The next model stepped out onto the runway, her dress the antithesis of the previous model.

Theo jerked beside me. "Is she—"

"No," I said, turning to cough into my fist to keep from laughing. "It's a body suit."

The nude-colored suit adhered to the model like a second skin, clutching and convulsing in a way that made it appear almost skin-like.

"Jesus," Theo muttered, a slight blush flushing his cheeks. "That's practically illegal."

I cocked an eyebrow. "I never took you for a prude."

"I'm not. I'm all about power to the people and feminism, and all that kind of stuff. I just never expected to see something like that."

The camera panned in on the suit, picking up the subtle sheen of crystals that dotted the fabric.

"Bold," Minerva enthused. "I could see one of our indie actresses strutting down the red carpet wearing this."

"I disagree," Alison said, shaking her head. "It's bold, yes. But it would be quite the faux pas to attend an event dressed as the award."

"I concur," Erike agreed. "They wear to draw attention, not become a laughingstock."

And so it went for another two couples before our model appeared.

"God," Theo cursed beside me. "You did it."

Sophia wore the crap out of the dress, strutting down the catwalk like Venus risen to tempt man. The dress moved with her, the light catching the faint sheen from the velvet and picking up on the dynamic fuchsia satin.

My heart pounded in my ears as the judges examined my design with their critical eyes.

Please like it, please, oh please like it.

"Now this is interesting." Alison leaned forward. "I love the contrast. It's sensual and playful while still being glamourous."

Theo caught my hand, squeezing.

"I'd have liked to see it with gloves," Minerva said, tipping her head to one side. "The train is clever, but the whole look could be elevated by gloves."

I absorbed her criticism while celebrating her praise.

"Mixed bag," Theo muttered.

"It's nothing new," Erike said dismissively. "Where is the innovation?"

I sagged, disappointed.

"Who needs innovation when you look like that?" Alison countered with a laugh. "I'm telling you, starlets will be lining the streets to wear a gown with that shape."

As quickly as the critique had begun, it was over, with only Keeley and Jude's design to come.

I breathed out a heavy sigh, relieved beyond words the ordeal was finally over. A strange mix of joy and disappointment warred inside me, churning in my chest.

"Could've been worse," Theo whispered, giving my hand a quick, reassuring squeeze. "At least we can't get voted off the island, right?"

"Small mercies," I muttered, managing a weak chuckle.

There were audible gasps as the next model stepped out. I glanced up, blinking in awe at their creation.

The talented duo had created a statement piece using crimson satin. It was a play on a tuxedo with a long ballgown skirt and a crisp short tuxedo vest top. The layering, the lines, the color—everything worked perfectly together to produce a showstopping dress.

"Damn," Theo said against my ear. "Correct me if I'm wrong, but that's a good design, right?"

I nodded mutely, my hopes crashing to the ground. It appeared the crew were correct in their assessment—Keeley and Jude were the team to beat.

The judges gushed over the design, agreeing that they had found their winner.

I applauded along with the other cast members as Keeley and Jude nodded, their expressions remote.

Damn. I really wanted to beat them.

"And now for our final surprise," Michelle said brightly into the camera.

I barely supressed a groan, slumping into Theo as the last of my energy drained from my body.

"You may be wondering why we were so specific with the challenge—and it's for a good reason." She turned toward the side of the stage. "Please welcome Beatrix Bellinger to the stage."

I shot up in my seat, my mouth dropping open as the woman herself walked out of the stage wings. Dressed in a costume from her latest movie, she glided across the stage, smiling a warm greeting.

"Welcome, Bea," Michelle greeted.

"Thank you so much," the actress responded, giving us a little wave.

"We like to keep our contestants on their toes, so why don't you tell us why you're here."

"I'd be delighted." She turned to the camera. "While the judges have picked their winner, I get to choose the dress I'd most like to wear to the Oscars." She chuckled. "As a nominee for Best Actress this year, I can assure you, your design will be seen by millions around the world."

My hands found Theo's, clutching him hard as my heart began to pound out of my chest.

"And I choose...."

CHAPTER 8
THEO

At what point do you decide to end a relationship?

Depends—is it an unsafe relationship? If so, now. If it's okay but not working for you anymore, then let it fade. If it's important to you, then fight for it

I hate that you're right

I always am. Unless you're talking about us in this scenario then the correct answer is never. I am legion

Thank God you're humble or you'd truly be unbearable

"I can't believe it," Mai repeated for the hundredth time as the elevator slowly ascended to our floor. "I cannot believe it."

"Believe it," I told her, grinning. "You're making a dress for Bea's Oscar appearance. I'm so fucking proud of you, Mai."

She jumped in my arms for another hug, beaming up at me. "I couldn't have done it without you."

I squeezed tight. "You did it *despite* me."

Mai slowly let me go and shook her head as the elevator doors slid open. "We did it together. Honestly, I'm in shock. This is so far beyond anything I could have ever imagined."

I pretended to hold a microphone. "Ms. Bellinger! Ms. Bellinger! Who are you dressed by tonight?"

I turned, switching the pretend microphone to my other hand, speaking in falsetto. "Only the winner of *Perfect Fit*, Ms. Mai Sakamoto, of course."

"Of course," Mai said, cackling. "There's no 'of course' about this. This is beyond my wildest dreams."

It hadn't surprised me that Mai's design would be chosen. One look at Beatrix Bellinger, and I'd known that our dress would look stunning on the actress—and I didn't even have formal training.

I pressed the key card against the door and sighed gratefully when it opened.

"Thank God they brought our bags up for us," I said, shoving the door open and holding it for Mai. "I'm ready to devour some greasy room service then hit the—"

I stumbled into her when she stopped dead.

"What are you—oh." I coughed. "I see."

A single queen bed stood in the middle of the hotel room, the pristine white bedding mocking us.

"Looks like the universe has a twisted sense of humour," I quipped.

"It's a couples competition," Mai said, her voice strangled. "They must have...." She glanced at me, and I relaxed seeing the amusement dancing in her eyes.

"I never even...." She giggled. "I can't—we—"

Belly-jiggling laughter burst from her, turning her into a silent clapping seal. Tears began to stream down her face as she bent over, gasping for air.

And, if I'm honest, I wasn't much better. The laughter exploded until I couldn't stand. Falling onto the bed, I dragged her down with me, setting off a new round of hilarity.

We were exhausted and pushed so far beyond our limits that at this point it seemed we were choosing to laugh rather than cry.

"I needed that," Mai said, swiping at her face between chuckles as she rolled onto her side beside me. "Do we ask for another room?"

I shook my head. "Don't want to inspire closer scrutiny."

"True." Mai sighed, her eyelids fluttering shut. "I'm too exhausted to think straight."

I brushed the hair back from her face. "How about I order us some room service while you hit the shower."

She sighed again. "But I want to sleep...."

"You know you'll never sleep if you don't wash your feet."

She chuckled. "True. I also can't remember how you know that."

"Our camping trip. You refused to get in a sleeping bag until you'd washed every inch of your toes."

"Some of us care about our hygiene." Groaning, Mai lifted into a sitting position. "Fine. But whatever you order, make sure there's a lot of it. I could eat an elephant."

I reached for the in-room phone as she kicked off her shoes and straightened them by the door.

The light in the bathroom switched on as I turned away, ordering us two giant pizzas, some garlic bread, and a side salad—I could be healthy when I wanted.

"And would you like any dessert?" the concierge asked.

I heard the shower turn on and glanced over as I answered. "No, that's—"

I spluttered, jerked out of my exhaustion by the unexpected sight of Mai's silhouette against the frosted glass of the bathroom wall.

"The... the shower wall is glass."

"Yes," the concierge said happily. "It's our best room for couples."

I hadn't taken a good look at the room when I'd entered, too focused on the one-bed situation. But now, as I glanced around, I could see what he meant.

The white wall I'd assumed was some kind of frosted glass feature was actually a semi-transparent wall that allowed the person on my side to see the outline of the person in the shower.

In one corner of the room sat a kinky-looking swing which, upon closer inspection, appeared to be less swing and more kink. Innuendo infused artwork featured on the other walls, while a small box beside the bed labelled "Essentials" listed its contents as condoms, silk cuffs, a blindfold, and small packets of water-based lube.

My gaze jerked back to Mai as she began to sing in the shower, her arms reaching over her head as she washed her hair.

My brain short-circuited as the shadowed outline of her body came into stark attention. I couldn't *see* anything—the frosted glass created just enough of a barrier to preserve her modesty. But the outline of her was more than enough to send me over the edge.

This is Mai! MAI! YOUR FRIEND, MAI! my internal voice screamed at me. *Look away! Look away!!!!*

"Sir?" the concierge asked. "Dessert?"

Spell broken, I jerked away, physically turning my back to the wall as I gulped in air.

"Nothing, thanks," I said, my voice hoarse.

"It will be up within the next thirty minutes."

We hung up, and I kept my back to the X-rated wall, trying to sort out my thoughts.

Thoughts? How about you sort out your physical reaction first?

My cock had joined the party of confusing messages my body had decided to throw at me.

I closed my eyes only to be assaulted by a vision of water sliding down Mai's skin as I pressed kisses to her shoulders, her neck, her mouth.

"Fuck," I groaned, jerking up from the bed to cross to the window. "Fuck, fuck, fuck."

Heat raged through my blood, turning me to fire. I pressed my forehead against the cool glass, fighting for calm.

Puppies in reindeer ears, Astipia losing the World Cup qualifying match, Annie when she's angry.

The fire in my veins slowly eased, leaving behind a throbbing, empty need.

Mai and I had been friends for far too long for me to be having this kind of reaction. She deserved more respect. She deserved a friend who wasn't tempted to perv, she deserved—

To be pressed against the glass and worshipped.

"Fuuuuuck," I groaned again, banging my head against the window. "What the fuck am I doing?"

It was fine. Totally fine. We were just friends, after all. Friends who touched now and then. No big deal. Friends who had kissed. Not a problem. Friends who were about to sleep in the same bed and pretend they were a couple, and maybe see the outline of each other's naked body.

IT WAS FINE!!!!

The shower switched off, but I didn't move, unwilling to subject myself to additional torture.

I heard the door open a minute later, and Mai stepped out of the humid bathroom carrying with her a warm waft of coconut-scented air.

"What did you order?" she asked, and I could hear her fiddling with her suitcase.

"Pizza." I cleared my throat, knowing I'd have to come clean. "Mai?"

"Mm?"

I swallowed and slowly turned to see her sorting through her things on the hotel floor. She wore a fluffy white robe that engulfed her, and on her feet were two tiny white slippers.

You have to be honest. Admit your trespasses and then ask for forgiveness.

Pulling up my big boy pants, I opened my mouth to do just that.

"Do you think they'll have actual food tomorrow?" Mai asked, pulling her toiletry bag from the depths of her suitcase.

"Probably. Mai, there's something I need to tell you."

"Is it about the bed? I've already decided I'll sleep on the floor."

I jerked. "You will not."

She waved a dismissive hand, still digging through her things. "It's not a big deal. I've slept in worse places."

I glanced at the bed. "We'll both be sleeping on the mattress. It's comfortable and gigantic. There's no need for either of us to get a restless sleep and put our game in jeopardy."

She glanced up, her cheeks flushed. "Damn, you're right." She sighed. "I guess we'll just have to hope one of us doesn't snore."

I snorted. "Babe, I already know you snore."

She tossed a sock at me. "No, I don't."

"Yeah, you do."

"How would you even know that?"

I lifted my hand, ticking off the ways on my finger. "Let's see, camping, vacations, that time you passed out on Ren's couch after breaking up with the she-witch."

Her lips twisted on that unpleasant memory. "Drunk snoring doesn't count."

"Oh, it does." I kept going. "Every time we go on a road trip, and you fall asleep within three hours of us starting—"

"I do not!"

"—the fact you slept on my shoulder on the plane."

She stuck out her tongue at me. "At least tell me I'm a cute snorer."

"Adorable," I agreed solemnly.

She chuckled, returning to her bag-digging. "What were you going to say?"

I glanced at the now-dark wall, briefly wondering if I could just avoid the whole conversation.

No way, pal.

"The wall is see-through."

Mai lifted a dress from her suitcase. "What wall?"

"The bathroom wall." I gestured at the glass. "Well, not exactly see-through so much as it's...."

How did one describe a peep show without the nips?

"Shadow puppet erotica."

Mai spluttered out a laugh. "What?"

Unable to explain without digging an even deeper hole, I pushed off the window, stepped around her, and moved to the bathroom. "It's easier if I just show you." I stuck my head back out the door. "And you have my permission to watch since I kind of did—though entirely by accident."

"Watch what?"

I switched the light on, grateful to see that—despite the voyeur wall—the rest of the bathroom appeared to meet the accessibility requirements we'd requested.

Walking gingerly over to the shower, I stood under the head, feeling awkward as I waved at the frosted glass.

"OH MY GOD!" came Mai's strangled screech. "Oh my God!"

I snorted. "No, just Theo."

"Not the time!" she yelled back.

I waggled my fingers, then turned them into a dog, then a bird, then a weird squid-thing. "Appreciate my puppetry of the hands—and not another appendage."

"Theo!"

I chuckled. "I'm going to shower."

I heard her say something but couldn't quite catch the words.

"What?" I called, pulling the adjustable bench from the wall.

"I questioned all that is holy."

I chuckled. "Baby, holy? Nah, this is Satan's work for sure."

Showering when you knew someone could see your outline had an entirely different feel about it—and my cock seemed to misunderstand the assignment. The prick bobbed up, slapping against my thigh as I tried—and failed—to ignore the itch on the back of my neck that reminded me that Mai stood on the other side of the thin partition.

I washed quickly and reached for a towel only to realize I'd made a fatal error—I'd forgotten to bring my crutch and clothes in.

Shit.

I pulled myself up to a stand, leaning against one of the assistant bars in the shower. "Mai?"

"Yes?"

I cleared my throat as I tied a towel around my waist. "Could you bring me my crutch, please?"

There was a long quiet moment before a soft knock sounded on the door. "Can I come in?"

"Sure."

Mai pushed the door open and stepped in, holding my crutch out in front of her.

Her gaze met mine, then dropped to the towel at my waist, her mouth falling open a little.

"Oh!" She flushed.

"Thanks." I took the crutch, shuffling toward the robe on the far side of the bathroom. "Sorry, I should have realized."

"No problem." Mai ducked her head. "I've already eaten. Do you mind if I brush my teeth?"

"Go ahead. I'll get changed in the other room."

I changed into a loose shirt and baggy gray sweats, inhaling the food that had arrived while I'd showered. Mai exited the bathroom after a few minutes and stood awkwardly by the bed.

"Swap?" I asked with a grin, tossing my plate onto the small table tucked in one of the corners of the room.

"Sure."

I brushed my teeth and checked the room lock, trying desperately not to think of Mai lying in my bed.

It had been an age since I'd slept beside anyone I found attractive. Damn if that didn't make me as nervous as a teen on prom night.

I paused at the end of the bed, surprised to see one very scruffy unicorn sitting on the bedside table.

"You brought Urma?" I asked.

Mai looked up from her book. "Of course. She's our good luck charm." She folded the corner of her page and tossed the book beside Urma. "Bed?"

"I'm not sure," I said, glancing pointedly at her novel. "Did I really just see you fold a corner?"

She rolled her eyes as she settled under the blankets, watching me move around the bed. "I forgot a bookmark."

"You're a monster and you know it."

Switching off the light beside the bed, I pulled back the covers and slipped between the sheets.

"Theo?"

"Mm?"

Mai sighed. "This is weird, right?"

"Totally." I turned my head to grin in her direction. "But weird isn't bad."

"No," she agreed. "It's not."

"Night, Mai."

"Good night, Theo."

And smiling, I fell asleep.

CHAPTER 9
MAI

MAI

Have you ever seen anything so beautiful?

THEO

Oh man, I'm already drooling

MAI

It is my greatest work to date

THEO

I'll be the judge of that. What flavors we talking?

MAI

I went with buttercream vanilla, peach and blueberry

THEO

Incredible! Did you design your dress to go with the cake or the cake to go with your dress?

MAI

You know me too well. The cake came after

THEO

A perfect pairing—kudos to you, master creator

My hands fed fabric through the machine as Theo distracted the camera crew, charming them with tales of woe and wonder. His interference worked for me, allowing me to concentrate on today's challenge and the designs we needed to achieve.

We had twelve hours to produce two designs for a swimwear brand. The winning designs would be featured in the brand's summer collection, with all profits going to a charity of our choice.

Now that I had one day of the challenge under my belt, the anxiety of the unknown had eased marginally.

Though, I couldn't say the same about my desire. Memories of Theo standing in just a towel assaulted me at the most awkward of times throughout the day, sending me into a blushing, bumbling mess.

It appeared that my curse of the unrequited crush had hit with a vengeance—and at precisely the wrong moment.

He's Theo. THEO! He's only being nice. The man isn't into you. Don't conflate your warm feelings of friendship with desire. It's not worth it.

Michelle interrupted my self-flagellation.

"I heard a rumor you and Mai have come up with a team name."

I snorted, glancing up from the machine. "I had nothing to do with it."

"She's right, it's all my genius," Theo puffed his chest out. "Are you ready for this, Michelle? I need to know if you can handle this awesomeness."

The host laughed. "I'm ready."

"Darn Knit All—with a k. Get it? Knit?" Theo chuckled. "Clever, right?"

Michelle shook her head. "Oh, that's positively horrid."

"I told you," I called, snipping a thread. "Don't encourage him. The puns will only get worse from here."

I realized my mistake when Michelle took my interaction as an invitation and came over—camera crew in tow—to observe the pieces I'd begun to assemble.

"This is interesting," she said, examining my sketch. "Tell me about it."

"We live on the coast in a little town called Capricorn Cove."

"North Island, right?"

I nodded. "My parents are second-generation Japanese

migrants and moved there for my mother's work. She's a marine biologist."

"Fascinating." Michelle touched the suit. "And this is for her?"

I nodded, feeling strangely emotional. "It was Theo's idea. He knows that some of my earliest memories are of watching my mother clean her wet suit at the end of each day."

I traced the embroidered pattern we'd created. "Whenever we faced any kind of life event she would say, '*mizu ni nagasu*,' which means 'the water flows.'" I ran my finger down the waterfall pattern Theo had designed, tracing the electric blue and red threads. "It's the equivalent of the English saying, 'water under the bridge.' I'm a naturally anxious person, and the reminder to let things go is a sentiment I appreciate, even if I don't always practice it."

Warm hands clasped my shoulders, squeezing gently.

I tipped my head back to grin up at Theo. "But we try, right?"

He nodded. "We always try."

Michelle sighed. "I love it." She tipped her head to one side. "How do your parents feel about you being on the show?"

I glanced at Michelle, wondering if she was asking because she was interested, or if she was falling into a biased opinion about potential conflict between my parents wanting a different career for their daughter.

"They're very supportive." I gestured around the table. "My grandmother was a seamstress. One could say I'm following in the family tradition."

Michelle grinned. "Oh, I like that. Do you have any examples of your grandmother's designs?"

"I do." Theo reached for his back pocket then chuckled. "Sorry, I forgot you guys made us hand over our phones."

Michelle chuckled. "I'll be sure to catch up with you later to see them. Good luck, you two." She left us alone at the table as the clock ticked down.

"I didn't know you had some of *obaasan's* designs."

He gave me a strained smile. "Why wouldn't I? Your grandmother is awesome. We text regularly."

I filed away that revelation for further examination as I raked my gaze over his face. "Are you okay?"

The lines at the corners of his eyes and mouth were pinched, a sure sign he wasn't.

"I need to sit down," he admitted, leaning heavily against the workbench. "And I wouldn't say no to some ibuprofen and a heat pack."

I hustled, grabbing one of the stools from under the table. "Sit, let me go see what I can find."

He gestured at the half-completed outfit. "But you need to finish."

"And we will—together and whole."

With a sigh, he took the offered seat without protest, his quick acquiescence setting off a fresh round of alarm bells.

Theo never did anything without protest—downplaying his pain and brushing off our attention with a smart comment or smile. The fact he wasn't protesting my hovering was a testament to how much he had to be hurting.

I searched out the medic who followed me back to our workstation.

"It's cramping," she said, after I gently bullied him into

letting her examine his thigh. "Likely from overuse. You need to rest and elevate it, if possible."

Theo tossed back the pain pills, stubbornly ignoring the camera crew who swarmed like flies around our table. "I'm fine, I just need to sit a minute."

The medic hummed under her breath. "If you're gonna force this then at least sit for the next hour. I'm not going to order you to leave the set, but I do want you to stay in the competition and the only way you'll do that is if you take appropriate rest breaks."

She ripped the back off a heat patch and gently pressed it to his scarred skin. "Promise me, rest."

Theo nodded, his jaw tight. I met Theo's gaze over the top of the medic's head. With a forced smile, he jerked his head at my machine. "Mai, time is wasting."

I didn't want to leave him, but the desperate, almost pleading look in his eyes sent me back to my seat.

"Fine," I said, forcing a lightness I didn't feel. "But I know you're faking to get out of this challenge."

He laughed, then groaned as the medic dug her fingers into the tight knot of convulsing muscle, massaging his flesh. "That's me—always such a drama queen."

I bent my head, forcing myself to focus on the task—and not the attractive man who sat in silent agony behind me.

"Thirty-minutes, designers!" Michelle called, sometime later. "And your models have arrived!"

The two models walked to us, both tall and lean. This time, we'd not had an opportunity to pick our model, instead they'd been assigned to us.

They dressed quickly and Theo directed the hair and

makeup artists while I completed last-minute hand pinning and stitching, ensuring that each part of the suit lay perfectly against their skin. I could tell it cost Theo dearly to be moving around as his face grew ashen. His laughter sounded forced, and his quips came slower as the clock wound down to zero.

"Tools down!" Michelle called from across the room. "It's time to strut!"

Thank God, I thought, pressing a hand to Theo's lower back.

"Are you okay?" I asked, my voice low.

"Let's just get through this."

We were once again whisked into the viewing room, and all my worry about the results of the competition dissipated as I sat next to a stoney-faced Theo. His fists were clenched on his thighs, his body held rigid as if a single touch would shatter him into a million pieces.

"What do you need?" I asked in a low voice.

"Pain relief. A crutch. For this to be over." A shadow of a smile touched his lips. "Don't worry, Mai. I won't embarrass you."

I opened my mouth to protest, knowing he could never embarrass me, but Michelle's entry music drowned out my protest. Instead, I laid a hand on his leg, hoping he'd understand through my touch what I couldn't communicate through speech.

The next few minutes were a blur of light, color, and fabric as models strutted down the runway and Erike, Minerva, Alison, and the founder of the brand discussed our creations. They got to ours and I could barely listen, my focus entirely on Theo.

"The fabric choices and mixture of textiles is divine," Alison enthused.

"I love the cut," Minerva agreed. "The fit for both models is stunning. And the way they've used the embroidery in both pieces to reflect that this is a cohesive collection is an act of genius."

"I am surprised that these came from Mai and Theo," Erike said, tapping his chin with a finger. "But I must concur. They seem to have found their rhythm. This is a collection I'd be happy to support."

The runway show came to an end, and we were mustered for the final announcements.

Hurry, I wanted to scream. *Theo needs rest.*

"The winner of today's competition is...." Erike paused for dramatic effect. "Mai and Theo."

I started, blinking as Theo pulled me into a tight hug, his delighted laughter hot against my cheek.

"You did it, Mai," he yelled, shaking me back and forth. "You won!"

I drew back to stare into his eyes, a startled giggle bubbling out of my throat. "Oh my God, oh my God!"

He pulled me back into him, squeezing me tight. "So fucking proud of you."

I gulped in air, holding him just as tight. "I couldn't have done it without you."

"Liar," he laughed.

We drew back a fraction, just enough that I could see Theo's bright eyes shining as he smiled down at me, his grin wide and sincere, even through his discomfort and pain.

An impulse overtook me. Before I could talk myself out

of it, I cupped his cheeks and caught his lips in a quick, soft kiss.

"Thank you," I murmured, pulling back to search his face for signs of rejection or repulsion. "I know how much today cost you."

"Don't mention it." He cleared his throat. "If this is my reward every time, then we better win more often."

I slowly let him go, sliding back to stand beside him.

After a tense few minutes, Bec and Meg Pezerczyk were eliminated.

"And then there were five," Theo murmured as we watched Bec and Meg exit the room.

We were dismissed and I helped Theo from the couch, supporting him as we moved through hotel toward the elevator bank.

We ran into our newly eliminated competitors in the lobby.

"Congratulations!" Bec said, swiping at her tears. "You deserved it."

"Thank you. I'm sorry you were eliminated."

She made a dismissive gesture. "Don't be. Swimwear isn't in our wheelhouse. It sucks, but we can hold our heads high and say we tried. Right, Meg?"

Meg nodded. "It's as much about the challenge as it is about the win."

"That's what people who lose would say."

I gasped, turning to see Keeley and Jude approaching.

"Geeze," Theo muttered against my ear. "Who pissed in their cereal?"

They reminded me of ice royalty—regal and aloof with Nordic features and ice-blonde hair. They were dressed alike in their signature high fashion suits they'd made from rich fabric hand-threaded by monks—or so I'd heard.

Keeley sniffed as she stood near us, staring down her nose at Theo.

I bristled, not liking this interaction one bit.

"Leave it," Theo warned gently. "They're not worth the energy pennies."

The elevator slid open, and we climbed into the car, shuffling to the back to make room for our fellow contestants. Theo stabbed the button for our floor then leaned against the wall, closing his eyes.

I bounced from foot to foot, willing the car to move faster. The silence inside felt deadly.

Keeley and Jude got off first, and we all sighed a breath of relief.

As they exited, I heard Keeley whisper a derogatory, ableist slur under her breath.

My head whipped around to pin her with a look. My anger rose, crashing with my need to protect Theo.

"Do you kiss your mother with that mouth?" I barked, scowling.

She crossed her arms over her chest. "I said nothing, little girl. Now run along so I can beat you tomorrow."

Theo chuckled. "Beat Mai? Nah. This woman is gonna wipe the floor with you." He squeezed my shoulders. "Come on, love. Let's get you to bed. I want to celebrate your win."

My anger took a brief back seat as Theo's lips brushed my cheek, his insinuation clear. But then he stabbed at the close door button, chuckling as it slid shut on Keeley and Jude, and my rage rose red-hot once more.

"I cannot believe," I growled. "How utterly, obnoxiously, outrageously, horribly—"

"I think that's enough descriptors," Theo said lightly.

"—rude that *woman* is!"

"Have you heard the rumor about them?" Meg asked.

I shook my head, watching Theo like a hawk. He'd begun to sweat, his jaw tense as the elevator slowly rose toward our floor.

"Rumor has it Jude's school flopped. They're broke and need the money to dig them out of the hole."

I winced. "That sucks for them."

Meg raised one shoulder in a half shrug. "Does it though?"

Theo snorted, a slight smile touching his cheek as we arrived at our floor. "Have a good night."

I slipped an arm around Theo's waist, helping him shuffle down the hall to our room. I swiped the pass on our door, as I helped Theo limp over to the bed. He groaned as he flopped onto the mattress, his hand dropping to his leg.

I sank to my knees beside the bed, still fuming as I automatically reached for Theo's shoe. He stared down at me as I undid his laces, still fuming.

"We have to beat those smug assholes." I tugged at his shoe, wrangling it off his foot as he began the process of removing his prosthetic. "I wanna wipe the floor with their stupid smirking faces."

"So bloodthirsty. This is a side I've never seen of you before. I like it."

I grunted, pulling his sock off and tucking it into his shoe. "I'm not normally provoked."

I placed Theo's shoe by the door, then took off my own, slipping into my room slippers with a sigh.

Theo popped some pills out of a blister packet and took a swig of the glass of water he'd left on the bedside table.

"How can I help?" I asked, watching him shift restlessly on the mattress.

"You know any acupuncturists who do house calls?"

I shook my head but held up my hands. "No, but I do know how to dig fingers in and rub."

He sighed, shuffling until he lay against the cacophony of pillows and cushions at the head of the bed. "I wouldn't normally say yes but...."

"Yes?" I asked, ensuring I had his permission before I touched him.

"Yes," he admitted softly. "Fuck, I hate days like these."

I crawled up the bed to settle beside his thigh. Gently, I rolled up the leg of his pants, pushing the fabric as high as I could get it without drawing it tight against his skin.

I'd seen Theo's scarring a few times but this felt different. Here he lay vulnerable and hurting as I placed hands on his skin and prayed I could help him.

The muscles felt like lumps of iron under my hands, thick and knotted as they pulsed with cramps.

"Let me get a hot towel." I moved to the bathroom, running one of the hand towels under hot water then wringing it out. I swiped up my moisturizer before returning to the bed.

He lay flat on his back, his pants removed and dressed only in his boxers and shirt.

"I can put them back on," he said, gesturing at his jeans.

"No, this is good. It gives me more access."

I handed him the damp towel, wincing at his gritted hiss.

I applied moisturizer to my hands, then lifted the cloth and tossed it on the side table.

"Don't judge me," he murmured as I began to gently knead his muscles. "I'm not Superman."

"I wouldn't want you to be." I bit the inside of my cheek as I found a particularly sensitive spot, causing Theo to grunt in pain.

"No?" he asked through gritted teeth. "Why not?"

I adjusted the pressure and angle, watching his face closely for signs of relief or pain.

"Superman is cool and all, but he'd never be around for birthdays or anniversaries. Saving the world is great, but every day? No thanks."

Theo tilted his head back, his fingers clenching in the bedsheets as the muscles under my fingers continued to cramp.

"Shit," he groaned. "Give me a second."

I paused, hating this for him. I wanted to take his pain and burn it into ash.

"Okay," he breathed finally, relaxing back on the bed. "I'm good."

He wasn't, but I appreciated his attempt to lie.

"How about you?" I asked gently after a long few minutes. My fingers moved, following the scarring on his leg. "You want a Wonder Woman?"

"Nah. I'm dating you."

I glanced up, finding Theo's gaze on me.

"Theo, I...." I swallowed, unable to speak but also unable to tear my gaze from his. Our mutual stare broke when I pressed on a particularly sensitive spot.

"Fuck," he swore, leaning down to grip his thigh. "Jesus that hurts."

Powerless to ease his pain, I could only continue to gently massage his convulsing muscles.

"I hate to say it," he sighed. "But I might need to break out a wheelchair tomorrow."

"Did you bring one with you?"

"No. I thought I'd be okay."

I bit my lip. "Should we organize one?"

"Let me just get through tonight and then we can work out if I need it tomorrow."

I nodded, swallowing my protest. I wanted to tell him it was alright, that everything would work out. I wanted to reassure him that I didn't need him to be anything but well.

But I knew his sense of responsibility and obligation wouldn't allow him to bow out of tomorrow's challenge.

I continued to massage his leg, moving up from the sensitive scar tissue that covered him from tip to mid-thigh, to the thick tendons in his upper thigh.

"Did I ever tell you about the incident?" he asked.

I paused, surprised by his question. He'd lain back on the bed, one arm under his head, the other fisted in a pillow on his stomach.

"No, I don't think so."

He stared at the ceiling. "You'd remember if I had, it's not a pleasant story."

I shifted on the bed, squirting more moisturizer onto my palm. "You don't have to share."

"I feel if you're dedicated enough to knead out the knots in my leg, then the least I can do is tell you how it got fucked up."

He shifted, stuffing another pillow behind his back. "Like all good stories, this one starts with evil parents."

I cocked an eyebrow. "I thought it was just evil stepmothers?"

"Not this one." He scratched his chest. "Once upon a time twin boys were born to a young couple. The man liked to drink, get high and cheat. The woman wanted to be a political mover and shaker, and married him simply because they were both silly enough to get knocked up."

He blew out a breath. "They didn't even last three years. The twins' third birthday was spent with their grandparents."

I winced. "I'm sorry."

"Don't be. Our grandparents loved us to distraction. How they raised a fuck-up like Walter, I'll never know." He huffed a laugh.

"Your dad had a history of being a not great guy?"

He nodded. "That's one way to put it. Guy had never heard of the word 'responsibility.'"

He winced as I touched a sore spot but continued. "I don't know if you remember, but I played ball in school. And I was good, really fucking good. We'd just won a game, and I'd been scouted. Everything was falling into place. Except Gramps had to go home early, and Linc needed our truck. I'd called him, but he never picked up. Instead of waiting, I accepted an offer from Walter. He'd been at the game." He shook his head. "I could smell the alcohol on him, but I'd thought, 'how bad could it be?'" He gestured to his leg. "That bad. He crashed us into a pole, rolled the truck, and walked away completely unscathed."

"I'm sorry."

He sighed heavily. "He's been sober for three years. And my guilty secret is, I fucking hate it."

I could hear the pain in his voice, see the tension and confusion in his face. "Why?"

"It's hard to hate someone when you respect them."

My heart ached for him. "You want to forgive him."

"Yeah." He closed his eyes. "He's good with the grandkids. Trying really hard to avoid using again. Which is another level of head fuckery for me."

"Because he didn't try when you got hurt?"

Theo's gaze met mine, a million unspoken emotions floating in their depths.

"Yeah."

I worked his leg, easing my way back down toward his knee. "Is there anything I can do?"

He shook his head. "No, I just... Days like today, when I'm in pain, it makes me want to rage at him. But I can't, you know? 'Cause he's trying to turn his life around. And I need to respect that effort."

"Doesn't mean you can't be upset."

"Mm." He sighed, then reached down to still my hand. "I'm good, Mai. Thanks."

"Anytime."

I cleaned up the cloths and lotion, and turned off the lights. Climbing into bed beside Theo, I felt like I'd managed to remove a little of the burden that had weighed him down.

"Thank you for sharing," I whispered into the dark.

His hand found mine under the blankets. "Thank you for understanding."

Smiling, I closed my eyes and drifted off to sleep.

CHAPTER 10
THEO

THEO

Do you know if there's an app for only fans?

MAI

As in the app literally called 'OnlyFans'??

THEO

No, I mean for hand fans. As in an app that celebrates the subtle skill of those who wield a hand fan

MAI

You've been watching Bridgerton again without me

THEO

I renounce your slanderous language! Good day, sir!

MAI

YOUR ACCOUNT SAYS YOU'VE ALREADY WATCHED THE WHOLE SEASON!!!!

THEO

I SAID, GOOD DAY!

MAI

This betrayal will not go unpunished

Waking up beside Mai had become a unique pleasure. I normally lived to sleep in, snuggled in the blankets, desperate to catch as many minutes as possible.

Not these days. These days, I woke early and just lay beside her, listening to her snore. Oh, the girl snored like a lumberjack. When we got home, I was totally enrolling her in a sleep study, it really couldn't be healthy.

But damn if it wasn't reassuring as fuck to hear.

In sleep, all the tension left her face, smoothing the little frown that had begun to carve out space between her eyebrows.

Slowly coming awake, I could feel that at some point during the night Mai had thrown a leg over my hip and snuggled into my chest. She'd migrated across the unwritten divide between our sides of the bed to cuddle into me.

And judging by how hard my cock felt right now, it appeared I didn't mind one bit.

She sighed, shifting in the bed as her mouth curved into a cute little smile. Her lashes fluttered, then settled, her soft snores resuming their reassuring rhythm. Unable to resist, I brushed hair away from her cheek, tucking it behind her ear.

Holding her like this felt like an intimacy that should be reserved for her lover.

Which I am not.

I sighed internally.

I wanted to deny that we were more than friends... but the reality was, Mai had begun to sneak her way out of the friendzone years ago.

I wanted to blame our kiss, or the kinky glass, or last night's confessional, but the truth was much harder to admit.

If I was brutally honest—which I always was in the few minutes before she woke—she may have been a large contributing factor in my dating downfall.

My dating history had a familiar pattern to it—meet person and charm them into a date, go on said date, and proceed to regale them with stories of Mai before pretending to be disappointed when they a) disappeared mid-meal, b) offered to be friends, or c) never called me again.

Rinse and repeat ad nauseam.

If Mai turned to me tomorrow and asked me out, I'd be all in. I couldn't pinpoint exactly when our friendship had grown to mean more to me, it simply had become so. But I needed to respect the relationship boundaries we'd established, and making shit awkward when she'd shown exactly zero sign of encouragement wasn't my style.

I'd had years of learning how to tuck my feelings away. Then we'd come here, where there was only one bed and the lines had become blurred. Not to mention that she'd begun showing a few signs of maybe beginning to see me as something other than a friend.

I just couldn't fucking tell if that was a result of the show or her growing to care for me.

Which led me back to the quiet of the mornings when I could torture myself with the fantasy that this fake relationship had become real.

Don't worry, I fucking hated myself for it.

As if hearing my thoughts, Mai stirred, her snoring cutting off as she yawned and snuggled closer into me, murmuring something nonsensical.

I grinned, watching her slowly blink awake.

"What time is it?" she asked, still mostly asleep.

"Nearly seven. We've got time."

She nodded, snuggling back into her pillow. "How's the leg?"

I shrugged. "I'll stretch it out today and try to be less active. It'll be fine."

She seemed to take me at face value, nodding once before her eyes grew heavy again. She shuffled—right into my erection.

I could tell the exact second she realized by the way she stiffened. Considering she'd taken up the whole bed, pushing me to the very edge, I couldn't exactly shuffle away. So I waited for her to react, curious if she'd pull away or shuffle closer.

"Theo?"

"Mm?"

She cleared her throat. "Are you—?"

"Of course." I chuckled. "I woke holding a gorgeous woman in my arms, Mai. What did you think would happen?"

She spluttered, her head tilting back to stare up at me. "But we're friends."

Her words plunged a deep wound in my chest.

Just friends.

I stuffed my feelings back into the little box I'd been storing them in for years.

"I know," I said, gently running my knuckles over her face. "Ignore him, he's got a horny mind of his own."

If this is all I'd ever experience, then I had to be satisfied. I couldn't push Mai to feel something for me if it wasn't there. She was far too precious a friend for me to fuck this up by making her feel guilty or obliged to try something with me based solely on my inability to keep my feelings to myself.

I began to withdraw, shifting to untwine myself from her when Mai's arms and legs tightened around me.

"Wait," she said, her dark eyes searching my face. "Maybe we could... cuddle? Just for a little longer?"

A shot of something that felt a lot like hope hit my bloodstream. I pulled her into my chest, holding her against me.

"Your heart is racing," she murmured into the quiet of the room.

I made a sound of agreement, unable to find the words needed to explain exactly why my chest thundered like a freight train.

I'm in love with my best friend.

She cleared her throat, then cleared it again. "You sure your leg is okay?"

"It's good." I flexed the muscles, wincing slightly at the

remaining tightness. "But I'll take my crutch to set today, just to be sure."

"That's a good idea."

We fell into companionable silence, our breathing beginning to match.

I wanted to kiss her. I wanted to admit how much I wanted to kiss her. It might change our friendship, but to hell with it—I wanted out of this purgatory.

"Mai, would you ever—"

Her alarm interrupted me.

With a sigh, I let her go, watching her roll over to tap on her screen.

"Would I ever?" she prompted, sitting up in bed.

"Never mind. Let's get ready for another day of competition."

Dressed and with stomachs full of hotel fare, we made our way down to the giant conference room once more.

There was something in the air today, a kind of brimming nervous energy that set my senses on edge.

"A double elimination," Michelle announced cheerfully as she outlined our next task. "This is a two-day challenge, and at the end of today, the team with the least creative vision, as decided by Erike, will be eliminated."

I exchanged a wide-eyed look with Mai.

"Yes," Michelle confirmed before anyone could ask. "We're looking for bold designs—meek and mild has no place in this competition."

Geeze, not even a chance to finish the design. Tough break.

"Tomorrow you'll present your final product for

judging. At which time, our judges will choose the top three teams to progress to the grand finale."

I glanced at Mai, raising an eyebrow. "I thought this gig was meant to go for six weeks."

She frowned. "So did I."

"Your challenge today is something a little different," Michelle said, a twinkle in her eye. "Today we're off to the Royal Gala. You may choose any of the themes from the long and vivid history of the event—and we can't wait to see which one you bring to life."

She turned to the clock. "Competitors, your time starts...." She paused dramatically. "Now!"

Mai and I took off for the textile area, my mind racing as I tried to remember themes from previous years.

Surprisingly, I did remember one.

"Wasn't there a year about Gods?"

"Heavenly bodies," Mai confirmed, her gaze sweeping over the multitudes of fabrics at our fingertips. "That was the year Robbie Huynh and his wife, Astrid, were crowned best in show."

"Wait, it's a competition? What do they win? Rich people yachts?"

Mai chuckled. "Not quite. They did look incredible though."

I glanced around, noting that the other contestants had already finished with their selections.

"What theme are we going for?"

Mai hesitated, then reached out to touch a bolt that seemed to be made of millions of sparkling tear drops.

"We're going to do Awakening Beauties," she said decisively. "I want a ballgown and the symbolism of the poisoned apple. We need to go with the romanticism and fantasy, the beauty and the drama."

I nodded. "Can we add the mice into this?"

"What?"

"You know." I held my hands up in front of my face, pretending to be a mouse. "Pumpkins and carriages, mice into horses."

"That's Cinderella."

"Shit." I held my arms out to accept the bolts of fabric she began to pull from the wall. "Which one has the bookstore?"

Mai snorted. "It's a library, and that's Beauty and the Beast."

"We're doing what one?"

"Sleeping Beauty."

I wracked my brains trying to remember which was which. "With the wicked stepmother?"

"I think the majority of them have wicked stepmothers."

I chuckled. "Is that a reference to our conversation last night?"

She offered me a wide-eyed look that failed in any way to look innocent.

"Gotcha." I thought about the many versions of fairy tales I had read over the years. "What if we did something different?"

Mai paused in her collection. "Like what?"

A concept began to take shape—something bold and a little bit left field. "Medusa."

"Medusa?" she repeated.

"Yeah." I juggled the bolts, suddenly overcome with

enthusiasm for my idea. "She's beautiful before her curse, but it's her rage that made her a legend."

"You know the horror of her story, right?" Mai asked, looking skeptical.

"Yep. Men are trash and the woman just wanted to be left alone. She turned guys to stone for being men. Going out on a limb, gonna say she was the first woman to choose bear over man."

Mai snorted. "Nah, that'd be Eve. Girl would have chosen a bear every time. Who do you think she was picking the apple for?"

I wiggled in place, practically vibrating with enthusiasm. "Coming back to the topic, her head was cut off, Mai. But what if this whole time she was just sleeping until we could bring her back to exact her final revenge? In dress form," I hurried to add. "You know, 'cause that's important."

Mai tapped one hand against her leg as she stared off into the distance. I could see the cogs in her mind turning over, thinking it through, creating and discarding ideas and designs.

"I... I can't believe I'm about to say this, but I really like it." She plucked the bolts of fabric from my arms, discarding them in an empty storage bin. "We need something that can start as one thing, then transform into another. We want her to be rising from her slumber—she is the snake in the garden of Eden, bringing Eve knowledge. She is the jezebel, Delilah, Lilith, and Maleficent. She is all the women who have been wronged." She laughed, shaking her head. "Theo, I am so into this idea. Thank you!"

She wrapped herself around me. She had aimed for my

cheek but at the last moment I turned my head, catching her lips by accident.

"Shit, sorry."

She pulled back, breathless and flushed, her eyes bright. We stared at each other, then she shook her head.

"Right, well." She cleared her throat. "We should get to work."

Mai's concept was daring, bold, and incredibly beautiful. She'd found a marbled silk that shimmered under the light. At first glance when pulled tight against the mannequin it looked like stone, but when loosened it became a shimmering dance of light.

We worked through the morning and into the long afternoon, pinning and folding, cutting and pressing, until a dress began to take shape.

Two hours before the end of the day, Erike began to make his rounds.

My lips curled, wanting to growl at him to go away as he stood over Mai, staring at her design.

"It's far from unique," he said dismissively. "A changing dress? Someone attempts it every year."

"But it's not just a dress," Mai protested weakly. "It's also about the story, which really speaks to—"

"Yes, yes, I know." Erike reached for Mai's pen, plucking it from her fingers to quickly sketch on the pad. "But here is your problem. There's rush in this dress, frantic stress." He handed her back the pen. "Breathe and try again."

Mai nodded mutely, watching him with big eyes as he left.

"Ignore him," I told her, wincing as I pricked myself once again. "He's a dick."

"He's one of the top designers in the world."

"My apologies. He's a *fashionable* dick."

She snorted, then bent over her drawing, considering the areas he'd circled. She sucked in a breath. "We'll just have to keep going until I work out how to give him what he wants."

What he needs is someone to tell him where to shove it.

I wisely kept that thought to myself.

"Contestants, you have thirty minutes of today's sew to go!" Michelle yelled from the platform at the front of the room. "And because we're not going to make this easy for you, we have another surprise."

Assistants streamed into the room to place boxes on our tables before walking away.

"You may now open your challenge box!"

I looked at Mai who seemed frozen, her fingers clasping a roll of satin.

"You want me to open it?" I asked, my voice low as cameras surged toward us, capturing every reaction.

She nodded, the color draining from her cheeks.

Around us were gasps and laughter, shrieks and sighs as the contestants unpacked their mysterious item.

With a flourish, I whipped open the box, shoving my hand inside to withdraw—

"Candles?"

"That's right, contestants!' Michelle swept across the platform, swirling in her gown. "It wouldn't be a Royal Gala without a little drama thrown into the mix. It's up to you to incorporate these items into your look!"

Around the room, each couple received something different. There were plates, napkins, even cutlery.

The candles toppled from my fingers to scatter across the workbench.

"Mai? What are you thinking?"

Silence.

Looking up at her, she seemed frozen, her eyes trained on the wax sticks.

"Mai?" I stepped closer, blocking her from the cameras. "You okay?"

She sucked in a deep breath, her head snapping back. "I... I...." She looked at me helplessly, tears glinting on her eyelashes.

Fuck.

I leaned in, covering my microphone with one hand, my lips brushing her ear. "Go. I'll distract them."

She nodded frantically, stepping back as the judges began to walk around the tables, drilling the contestants on how they were pivoting their designs.

"Candles!" I boomed, swinging my arms wide and shooting the camera a cocky grin. "Are they expecting us to set the dress alight? That would certainly be memorable." I grabbed my crutch and powered toward the fabric area, forcing the camera operator to follow me as Mai slipped away.

"Don't worry, Mai! I'll check which fabrics aren't flammable!" I stopped at the fabric rolls, reaching out to finger a piece of flannel. "After all, we want Medusa not *cinder*-ella."

Celeste shot me a thumbs-up, her grin large and ecstatic. As predicted, I'd managed to win her over through good cheer, lots of puns, and a shit-ton of coffee hand-delivered to her each morning.

I glanced back at our table, grateful to find that Mai had disappeared and the countdown clock was minutes away from ending our day.

Filling time, I walked around the materials, joking with the camera and generally getting in the way of the other contestants and crew until Michelle blew her whistle, halting the day's work.

"See you tomorrow, contestants!"

With a long sigh, I switched off my microphone, handing it over to my handler.

"Where's Mai?" I asked, my voice low.

"Dressing room. She's...." He shook his head. "Not great."

"Are they recording her?"

"No." He glanced around, then leaned in, his voice low. "I told them her microphone had fucked up. They agreed to let her end the day early rather than deal with swapping it out."

I clasped his shoulder. "Thanks, Greg. I appreciate your discretion."

"No problem. My brother lives with anxiety. I recognize the signs." He nodded at someone over my shoulder. "I'll see you tomorrow."

"Thanks."

Using my crutch, I made my way to the dressing room, my steps echoing in the empty hallway. Pushing open the door, I found Mai sitting on a stool, her head bowed, hands fidgeting with a loose thread on her pants.

"Hey," I said softly, leaning against the doorframe. She looked up, her eyes tired.

"Hey," she replied, a hint of a smile touching her lips.

I walked over and sat beside her, stretching my legs out in front of me and placing my crutch on the floor. Turning, I gave her a comforting squeeze on the shoulder. "You did great today, you know that?"

Mai let out a shaky breath. "I feel like I'm falling apart. This competition is so much harder than I thought."

"It's okay to feel overwhelmed," I reassured her. "But remember why you're here. You have a gift, and you deserve to showcase it."

She nodded slowly, but still clearly unsure. "It's just...." Tears shimmered on her lashes. "I don't know if I can do this, Theo. Everything is just so intense. Every time I feel like I'm on top of it, they throw something new at us and I become—" She gestured at herself.

"Perfect?"

She shook her head, not even summoning a laugh. "I'm a hot mess."

I pulled her head against my chest, holding her tight against me. "You're not."

"I am."

"Fine. You are. But so what? Aren't we all hot messes?"

She tilted her head back to look up at me. "No. You're completely together."

"If you believe that then I'm doing a better job at pretending than I anticipated. Feeling your emotions isn't a bad thing. For a long time post the crash I struggled to feel anything but anger." I looked down at our clasped hands. "We're told by society to be meek and mild and gentle. To hold space for our emotions but only show them in private—or at a ball game. We're judged if we cry too much or not enough. We're told to not burden people but to admit when we need help. You know what? I'm fucking sick of it."

I looked down into her stunning brown eyes. "Just be you, Mai. And if the you you need to be right now is a crying, sobbing wreck of a human being, so be it. I don't care. You're still going to be one of the best people I know—snotty nose and all."

She stared at me for a beat. "Theo?"

"Yeah, babe."

"I'm going to squeeze you right now."

I pulled her closer. "Squeeze as long as you want."

And there in the quiet of the dressing room, the little box that had contained my feelings for Mai began to fracture.

CHAPTER 11
MAI

Got any great porn recommendations? I'm in the mood for something spicy tonight

I appreciate you trusting me with this new step in our friendship. Alas, no. Not really. I tend to get my jollies off while reading books. There's something about being able to connect so deeply with the characters that really gets me going

Though, now that I think about it, I don't mind a good slow and sensual massage video or two. But it has to be genuine connection couples not, wham bam thank you ma'am. I'm really picky

PORK!!

PORK RECOMMENDATIONS!!!

I BOUGHT PORK!!!!! PORK!! I WANTED SPICY PORK RECIPES!!

FUCKING AUTOCORRECT!!!

> But since we've started down this track....
> Have you tried erotic ASMR?

We lived to fight another day. Erike eliminated Alec and Tempest De Soto. The weight of our own survival pressed heavily on my chest, as if my heart threatened to burst through my ribcage. My fingers trembled as I clutched the sketchbook in my hand, seeking solace in the familiar pages.

Come on, Mai. Think!

After a grueling day of filming, we'd retreated to the sanctuary of our hotel room. Theo had ordered room service, and now we sat huddled over the small table, surrounded by scattered papers and design tools. I needed to rework our design to incorporate a candlestick. Its inclusion had become a crucial element that would determine if we'd make it through to the grand finale. The pressure felt suffocating, weighing on me with an intensity I couldn't ignore.

Desperate for inspiration, I'd lit a few of the candles, hoping they might spark an idea. But alas, my mind remained blank.

Pressure is on. You need to get this right to get into the grand finale. Everything is riding on this, Mai. Everything.

"I have an idea," Theo announced, tapping a pencil against the tabletop.

"I'm glad someone does." I pushed away my paper, running fingers through my hair. "Shoot."

"They're expecting fire, right?" He dropped the pencil

and ran his fingers over the top of the flame of one of the candles. "What if we did the opposite and used the wax?"

I wrinkled my nose in confusion. "Wax and clothing?"

"No." He lifted the black candle with one hand, holding it six inches above his opposite wrist. "Wax and skin."

He tipped the candle on its side, and I watched as a droplet of wax pooled before cascading over the edge to land on the sensitive skin of his inner wrist. He sucked in a breath, his teeth catching his bottom lip.

The interplay of the dark liquid against his light skin, the way the flame flickered and danced as more wax slowly fell to cover his arm in a patchwork pattern of droplets... It all coalesced to unlock a deep, unexpected need in me.

I want to feel that.

I licked my lips, my gaze trained on the falling wax. "Doesn't it hurt?"

"Not if you do it right."

I glanced up, meeting his dark gaze. His eyes held a new intensity, and in them. I read a hunger and need that mirrored my own desires.

Oh.

Our dynamic had changed. I could see it in his gaze, feel it in his touch. An intimacy now existed, new and fragile but building.

I liked it, even if this change terrified me.

I silently scolded myself, attempting to regain control over my racing thoughts.

"W-what is your idea?" I asked, desperate to cut the tension between us.

"We were planning on putting her in lace gloves, right?"

I nodded.

"Here, let me show you what I'm thinking."

He replaced the candle in its holder and held out a hand, wiggling his fingers. "Give me your hand, Mai."

With only the slightest hesitation, I slid my palm against his, sucking in a breath when his warm fingers closed around mine.

"Watch."

He reached for one of my silver markers, pulling off the cap with his teeth. A hot liquid shimmer pooled low in my abdomen, reacting to the strangely primal move.

This is Theo. Your friend. YOUR FRIEND!

"What if..." Theo murmured, bending over my hand. "We do something like this?" With slow, gentle strokes, he ran the silver gel pen over my skin.

I tried to ignore my reaction to his touch. Tried not to catalogue the multitude of sensations that sparked at every glide of the pen and brush of his fingers.

"Are you cold," he asked, his voice a low whisper.

"No," I answered, my tone similarly hushed. "Why?"

He paused to brush his pinkie over my forearm. "Goose bumps."

"I—"

How did one find the words to describe the pleasant tingles that shimmied from my head to my toe?

"It feels nice."

He made a sound in his throat—an affirmation? A groan? An acknowledgement? —and dropped his head to continue drawing.

The pen swirled, creating an intricate latticework representation of an elbow-length glove.

"Now," Theo murmured, setting the pen to one side. "We add the wax."

With gentle, deliberate movements he lifted the black candle, holding it aloft. He tipped it, sending a single drop to slash down against my skin.

I hissed as the warm liquid latched on, shuddering when Theo blew on it, helping the wax adhere to my skin.

"Too hot?"

I shook my head, my eyes closing as I gave in to the multitude of sensations assaulting me.

The flash of heat had reduced but still lingered. The pinch of the wax as it hardened. Theo's firm grip as he slowly rotated my hand, covering it in a multitude of droplets. His warm breath as he blew against my wrist.

"There," he eventually murmured, releasing his grip on my hand. "What do you think?"

I forced my eyes open, struggling to pull myself free of the pleasant tingling state of relaxation he'd created.

"Oh." I touched the edge of a wax droplet. "Theo, this is gorgeous."

He'd turned mere wax and pen into an elegant Victorian-lace glove. Turning my hand this way and that, I couldn't help but envision how this would look when paired with our steampunk-princess-rescues-herself dress.

"It's perfect."

He grinned, flicking hair out of his eyes. "I'm occasionally useful."

He reached for my undecorated hand.

"What are you doing?"

His thumb brushed the soft pad of my palm. "Your other side." He reached for the pen. "You good with that?"

I swallowed hard as a deep ache began to pulse in my abdomen; my gaze fixed on his as I summoned my courage.

"Yes."

He bent over my hand, his breath warm as it brushed my overly sensitive skin. My eyelids drifted closed, my body relaxing under his attention.

"Mai?"

"Mm?"

"You ever think about me?"

His words hung in the space between us.

I opened one eye, peeking out at him. "Of course."

Theo's head remained bowed; his focus trained on creating the intricate pattern on my hand. Silence stretched between us before he finally set my hand down on the small table. His head lifted slowly, his gaze locking with mine.

Slowly, deliberately, he reached for the pen lid. I watched as he clicked it back on and returned the pen to my stationery bag.

"What I mean is," he said slowly, as if trying to pick his way across a minefield. "You're my best friend, Mai. You're intelligent, resilient, strong, generous and gorgeous. I love how much you make me laugh, and how much we laugh together." He took my hand, stroking my pulse point with his thumb. "But there's a catch. As much as I love being your friend, I can't shake this idea that we could be more. You're constantly on my mind, Mai. You're the first thing I think of when I wake, and the last before I go to sleep."

He hesitated, glancing down at our clasped hands. I waited, my heart in my throat as he seemed to collect his thoughts. Then Theo's eyes flashed with determination. He rose, pulling me up to a stand.

"If you don't feel the same way, I understand. But I want to lay it out there because the idea of spending my life with you, of exploring if we could be more, of laughing with you—it's something I'll forever regret if I don't take this chance."

He gestured at the room around us. "This isn't the perfect time, I get it. And if this makes you uncomfortable, then I'll organize another room to stay in. There's no pressure here. This is your decision. I'll understand either way."

I swallowed, stunned by his confession. My heart pounded in my chest, my stomach tight as my breathing grew shallow. Time seemed to stop as we stared at each other, the weight of our unspoken feelings hanging in the air.

He gave me time, watching as I processed his declaration.

"Have you felt like this for a while?" I asked, my voice hoarse.

He huffed out a laugh. "You could say that."

I glanced away, trying to sort through the multitude of thoughts and feelings running through my brain.

My eyes caught on the ring on my middle finger and all doubts faded.

Straightening, I looked up at him, needing him to see how clearly I made this decision.

"You're my best friend. I love our text messages and the way you make me laugh. I love how you're strong and courageous, but kind of a goofball. I love the way you care to learn about the people in your life. I love how you adore your niece and nephew, and know exactly when Linc and Annie need a night off. So, yes. I'm in."

He blinked. "Do you mean—?"

I reached up, wrapping my arms around his neck and standing on tiptoe.

"I mean," I said with a laugh, "kiss me."

"Fuck yes." His head bent until his mouth hovered mere breaths above my own. "For the record," he said, his whisper hot against my lips, "I'm consenting to everything."

Our mouths collided, hungry and desperate. The walls around our attraction seemed to burst as years of pent-up tension ignited.

Theo shifted, deepening our kiss, his tongue teasing mine as his hands brushed over my back. My fingers slid into his hair, tugging him closer.

I wanted his hands on me, his fingers in me. I wanted him touching and caressing, teasing and taunting. I wanted him today, tomorrow, every day.

Unlike most decisions in my life, this felt easy. I'd expected panic but instead felt oddly at peace, a wash of calm and the feeling of coming home settling in me, body, heart and mind.

His fingertips danced across my skin and I lost myself in the sensation. I adjusted the angle of our kiss to nip at his lip, and relished his guttural groan.

The newness of our embrace mixed with the familiarity of Theo to become a strange riptide of languid, delicious lust.

Theo.

His hands slid down my back to settle on my hips,

yanking me closer. I groaned at his possessiveness, relishing the way he made me feel.

Our tongues danced together, exploring each other's mouth with a near desperate hunger. God, how long had this been brewing? How long had it been simmering under the surface, both of us too afraid to act.

"You have no idea how long I've wanted to do this," he murmured against me between kisses. "To touch you, taste you."

I tangled my free hand in his hair, tugging him up until his face was level with mine, our breath mingling. "Kiss me."

"Gladly."

His mouth returned to mine, hot and demanding. I opened for him eagerly, desperate for more.

He shuffled us until my thighs hit the edge of the table. With a sweep of his arm, he sent the candles and papers scattering to the floor. Then he lifted me, laying me out on the tabletop like a pagan offering.

"Wait! Your leg!"

"Fuck my leg," he growled against my mouth. "It's not the part of me aching right now."

I'd always assumed Theo would be a gentle lover, mixing humor with sensual teasing. Instead, he became a dominant frothing beast, controlling me and my body even as he lost his self-control.

I loved it.

"You're overdressed," he growled, eyes raking over me. His hands found the hem of my shirt and ripped it over my head. My bra quickly followed, baring me to his hungry gaze.

"Fuck, look at you," he groaned, cupping my breasts in his large hands. He rolled my nipples between his fingers and I cried out, arching into his touch. "Fucking perfect."

"Theo," I whispered, and his gaze flicked up to meet mine. In their depths, I saw my own need reflected back at me, raw and undisguised.

"Let me make you feel good."

I swallowed, nodding as anticipation unfurled in my belly.

"Words, Mai. I need the words."

"Yes. Please."

His dark chuckle danced across my skin as he lowered his head to my breasts. I gasped as I felt his tongue, hot and wet, tracing the delicate flesh of my areolas. He laved my skin, his teeth grazing gently as bolts of pleasure shimmied down to pool deep in my abdomen.

"I want to taste all of you," he rumbled against my breast. "I want to see you covered in my marks."

A broken moan escaped me at the thought. "Yes."

To my surprise, he withdrew, reaching for a candlestick. I watched, swallowing as he relit the snuffed wick, then held it over my chest.

"You liked me decorating your skin, didn't you, Mai?"

I nodded breathlessly, watching in anticipation as the wax pooled into a single drop, hovering on the edge.

"I'm going to cover you in wax, pretty girl. Then lick you until you come."

I shuddered at his erotic words, hardly able to reconcile that this man was the same person I'd spent the last few years teasing.

The first drop of wax hit my skin, hot and stinging. I

gasped at the sensation, back arching involuntarily as the sting faded to a cool warmth. Theo grinned down at me, a wicked gleam in his eyes.

"You like that, baby?" he purred, tipping the candle to spill more wax onto my chest. Each drop sent a jolt of pleasure-pain through me, heightening my arousal.

"God yes," I panted, writhing under his ministrations. "More, please."

Theo obliged, creating intricate patterns across my breasts and down my stomach. I'd never been someone into anything even remotely kinky, and yet here I was, a puddle of sensation, my world narrowed to the slide of hot wax on my skin and Theo's intense growls of praise.

"Fuck, you're stunning."

This man is a danger to my heart.

The thought coasted over me, flitting away as he gently dotted my torso, creating an elaborate artwork. By the time he was satisfied, my underwear was soaked and pleas seemed to stream from my lips in a never-ending cycle.

Theo blew out the candle and set it aside. "Beautiful," he murmured reverently, lowering his head to lick my erect nipples. "You're gorgeous, Mai."

His hand trailed down my torso, soothing my overly sensitive skin. He rested his palm on the edge of my pajama pants and waited.

"Yes," I said, arching up toward him. "Please."

Together, we shimmied the pants down my legs until I was left in just my underwear.

Theo kissed his way down my body, nuzzling the sensitive skin of my inner thighs. He hooked his fingers in the waistband of my underwear and looked up at me again, silently asking for permission. I nodded frantically, lifting my hips so he could slide them off.

As he tossed the material over his shoulder I realized the height of the table would be a problem for him to kneel on his leg. Pushing up onto my elbows, I opened my mouth to suggest we move to the bed but Theo beat me to the punch.

Hooking his arms around my thighs, he lifted my bottom off the table and bent until his mouth was on me. Gasping, I slumped backwards as his clever tongue explored, teased, and tasted turning me into a quivering, moaning mess.

His fingers found my core, teasing my entrance as his tongue flicked over my clit. I cried out, my hands fisting in his hair as I tried to pull him closer to get more of his sinful mouth on me.

"Patience, Mai," he chuckled against my skin. "I want to savor you."

He slid one long finger inside me, stroking in time with the licks of his tongue. My head fell back against the table, lost in a haze of pleasure as I surrendered to the sensations.

Theo added a second finger, curling them to hit that perfect spot inside me. I writhed beneath him, gasping his name like a prayer as the tension coiled tighter and tighter.

"That's it, baby, let go for me," he encouraged. "Ride my face, filthy girl. Take what you want."

His tongue returned to my clit and I shattered, my body shaking with the force of my release. Theo worked me through it, drawing out my pleasure time and time again until I finally begged him to stop, unable to take any more.

Gently, he helped me off the table and shuffled us over to the bed.

I curled on the quilt cover, panting, shellshocked, unable to comprehend how this man—this beautiful golden retriever of a man—had turned into a fucking wolf in the bedroom.

He disappeared, and I could hear the sound of running water. When he reappeared, he held a small tube of something in one hand and a washcloth in the other.

"Let me take care of you," he murmured, gently rolling me onto my back.

With tender hands he removed each drop of wax, gliding the cool cloth over my sensitive skin. He followed with little dots of aloe vera.

"Did you plan this?" I asked, touching the tube of gel.

"God no." He held it up. "I always carry this in my toiletries. You never know when you might end up sunburnt to shit." His gaze dropped to my dotted chest. "Or apparently in a wax-play situation."

We exchanged a grin, and it felt weird that this didn't feel weird.

But I was too exhausted to care.

"Will I have marks tomorrow?" I asked, touching the remnants of a wax drop on my wrist.

"You shouldn't. We used soy wax, and it wasn't very hot." Theo disposed of the cloth and gel, then returned to the bed, handing me my recovered pajamas.

Flushing, I pulled them on while he removed his prosthetic. I slid under the bed sheets, watching as he set up his bedside for the next morning.

He slid under next to me, then caught my expression.

"Hey." He cupped my chin in his hand. "You okay?"

I sighed. "Not really. I feel pretty bad that I got all the

attention." I gestured at where Urma sat, her brown eyes staring out at the room. "Not to mention the bad example we're setting for Urma."

He began to chuckle, which escalated to full-on laughter.

Mock-frowning, I lifted up in bed to glare down at him.

"I'll apologize to Urma. Maybe get her some earplugs and an eye mask or something." He tugged me down on him. "But seriously, Mai, I haven't come like that since I was a teenager."

I spluttered against his chest, lifting my head to stare at him. "No jokes?"

"No jokes. You turned me on that much." He kissed my nose. "I'm good, Mai. Promise."

Relieved, I snuggled into his chest. "Well, I won't apologize for my magnificence."

"Never apologize for that." His chest rumbled against my ear with his chuckle.

"We should sleep," I murmured, enjoying our closeness.

"We should," he agreed easily.

"You need to rest your leg."

He made a non-committal sound.

Yawning, I reached over his shoulder and turned off his bedside light. "Rest it," I told him. "And tomorrow we might try that again."

I fell asleep to his quiet laughter.

CHAPTER 12
THEO

I awoke slowly, enjoying the feel of the woman in my arms. Nuzzling her hair, I held her close, pressing lazy kisses to her shoulder.

"Theo?"

"Mm?" I mumbled, my voice thick with sleep.

"Did you rest your leg?"

I became aware of her soft lips touching feather-light

kisses along my chest. Blinking the sleep from my eyes, I registered gentle hands caressing my thighs.

"Um...." I mumbled, my voice thick with sleep. "What are you doing?"

I felt her smile against my skin, her breath warm as her tongue swirled around my nipple. "I promised we'd try again if you rested." She tilted her head back, giving me a pouting look. "Did you rest?"

My cock hardened. "Yes."

Her smile reminded me of sin. "Good."

She gently disentangled herself from my arms to squirm under the blankets and dance her mouth down my body, her tongue teasing and stroking as she went.

"Babe, you don't have to," I protested weakly, gathering her hair in my hands under the blanket.

I felt her hot breath against my cock. "I need the words, Theo," she teased, echoing me from last night.

With a groan, I tightened my grip on her hair. "Fucking yes."

She took me into her hot, wet mouth in one smooth move.

My brain might have taken a minute to catch up, but my cock stood ready to do his duty.

Curses rained down on her as I struggled to breathe, her wet heat fully engulfing my erection.

"Oh fuck," I gasped, as she swirled her tongue around my crown. "Jesus fucking Christ."

I threw off the blankets to reveal her gloriously naked body crouched between my thighs.

God, she was beautiful.

Her black, sleep-mussed hair stood in tufts here and

there, adorably wild. The angry red marks of the previous
night had faded, leaving behind a light shimmer of aloe on
her dark skin. Her mahogany eyes looked up at me, teasing
me as she ran her tongue around my cock.

Propping up on my elbows, I watched her, mesmerized
by her confidence. Early morning light filtered through the
curtains, casting a soft glow over Mai's naked body as she
worked my length.

Smiling, she held eye contact a moment before she took
me deep, the tip of my cock hitting the back of her throat.

"Fuck!"

I dropped back on the bed, burying my hands in her
hair. "Come ride my face while you do that."

She started, and I could tell she wasn't sure.

Ignoring her uncertainty, I crunched up, hooked my
arms under her, and dragged her off my cock and up
the bed.

"Theo!"

"On my face," I demanded, helping her shuffle until she
was in reverse cowgirl position.

Humming happily when she finally complied, I gripped
her hips, lowering her down.

"Good girl."

She bent, wrapping her mouth around my cock as I
licked up her slit, savoring her sweet, musky taste. I fucking
loved how she shuddered at the touch of my tongue, how
she moaned around my cock as I began to work her sensitive
folds with my mouth.

"You taste amazing," I murmured as I swirled my
tongue around her clit. She whimpered and took me deeper,
sucking me hard as her hips rocked against my face.

I focused my attention on her clit, licking and sucking while she writhed above me, her thighs clamping down around my ears.

Fuck yes.

Her moans vibrated deliciously around my shaft as I built her up, pushing her closer to the edge. With a shuddered gasp, my cock popped free of her mouth as she arched back, rocking against my tongue.

"Right there," she panted, fisting my cock in time with her rocking. "Don't stop, don't stop, don't stop!"

Gripping her hips tighter, I feasted on her like a man starved, licking and sucking greedily as her thighs trembled. She cried out as her orgasm crashed over her, flooding my tongue with her taste. Growling, I thrust up into her hands, fucking her fingers until I came.

"Fuck."

She flopped forward on the bed, rolling to lay beside me, her head by my foot. I entwined our fingers as we panted, both of us wrecked by our releases.

"Shit," I muttered, slowly rolling over to stare at her. "That was not how I expected to be woken up today."

She chuckled. "Well, good morning to you."

"And to you, Ms. Sakamoto."

I captured her legs, dragging her up the bed and spinning her around as she squealed until I could gather her in my arms. Our first kiss of the morning was slow and easy, full of gentle reverence.

We cuddled, exchanging soft, slow kisses, our hands gently exploring but not igniting. After the craziness of the last few days, this slowdown felt right.

I gently brushed a lock of hair from her face. "What do

you want to do today? We could stay in bed all day, or go grab some breakfast, or go win a competition. I'm also open to marriage proposals."

Surprisingly, I was only half-joking about the proposal.

She giggled, idly tracing patterns on my chest with her fingertip. "Hmm, breakfast does sound good to start." She sighed. "We have to finish today's challenge."

I touched my finger to a stray piece of wax on her arm. "You think we're not going to win?"

She shrugged. "I think we'll do our best."

"Then that's all that matters, right?"

She nodded, remaining silent as she continued to trace patterns across my chest.

"Hey." I waited until she looked at me before continuing. "We're getting to the grand finale."

Her lips twisted. "You're far more confident than I am."

I wished she had more faith. Mai was too fucking talented to underestimate herself.

"I'm too ignorant to be intimidated," I corrected. "When you don't understand the stakes, it's easy to be fearless."

Kissing her once more, I reluctantly disentangled myself and rolled to the edge of the bed. "C'mon, beautiful. Let's go fuel up. We're going to need the energy." I reached for my crutch, then hauled myself up and out of the bed.

Mai laughed. "I'll hold you to that, mister. Now, do you want to join me in the shower or watch the show?"

This was definitely a win-win situation.

I gave myself permission to trail my gaze down the length of her as she lay in bed, a teasing smile on her swollen lips.

My jaw clenched at the sight of her curves, her skin, her dark nipples, the little thatch of black hair between her thighs.

I wanted to fuck her on every surface of the hotel room. I wanted to tease her slowly, making love to her until we were both mindless and desperate. I wanted to savor the build, revel in the anticipation until both of us burned with need.

I'd become so used to jumping into things without thought that to pause seemed almost counterintuitive. But then I'd never been playing to win Mai's heart.

"Shower," I said definitively. "I want you on my lap while I make you come once again."

She swallowed. "Will we...?"

I shook my head. "Not yet. But we will. I want to savor the buildup a little longer."

"Oh, you're dangerous." She waggled her finger at me. "I should be calling your exes to get the lowdown on you."

I grimaced, following her into the bathroom. "Please don't. I might be friends with a few, but they're bound to tell you all the dumb shit I've done over the years."

"I already know half of it." She pulled the bench seat down and moved out of my way as I transitioned into the shower.

"And I'm glad you only know half."

She chuckled as I turned on the overhead shower. Stepping into the water, Mai climbed up on the bench seat, straddling my thighs.

"Ready?" she asked as water dripped down her gorgeous body.

I slid a hand between us, finding her wet heat.

"For you? Always."

———

We made it to the studio with two minutes to spare. Sound technicians frantically miked us up as makeup artists and hair stylists fought to make us TV worthy.

We took our places with the other contestants, and I could feel the nervous energy. It appeared everyone was keenly aware of how much was riding on today.

I caught Mai glancing at my leg and sighed.

"I told you, it's fine."

She bit her lip, flushing. "I know. You know your body best. I'm sorry."

I leaned in, brushing my lips against her ear. "You're forgiven if you do that thing with your tongue again tonight."

I chuckled as her face flushed.

"Contestants," Michelle called from her place on the stage. "You have just eight hours left to complete your look fit for a royal. Go forth and create!"

"I'll do the gloves," I said, already planning the structure.

"You're not just applying straight to skin?" Mai asked, checking the fabric pieces she'd pinned to our mannequin the day before.

"No, I had an idea while you were washing my co—er," I coughed, remembering the microphone tapped to my chest. "While you were washing my *sock*."

I could see her shoulders shaking as she bent to pin the skirt on the mannequin.

"What was your idea?"

"I want to create a melted wax glove." I held my hand out, cupping my palm. "If I use a thin band of wire and canvas that slips around the model's hand, the wax should melt onto it."

Mai tilted her head to one side, tapping a finger against her lower lip. "How does that fit with the dress?"

"I'll make the wave look like stone. We'll rig the cords of the skirt to the gloves so when the model opens her arms, the cord will pull to reveal the full skirt."

We'd designed this piece to look like a skin-tight dress until the wearer tugged at the clever hidden ties and released the full skirt into the train—turning the dress from stone to water.

"I'm not sure I completely understand, but I'm happy to give it a try."

"Trust me," I told her confidently. "It'll work."

It didn't work.

The wax warped the wire frame, and dripped off the canvas before it had a chance to set. I cursed under my breath, trying to salvage the mess—and contain it to my small corner of the workbench. Mai glanced over, her brow furrowed in concern.

"I'm sorry," I said sheepishly. "It sounded good in theory."

Mai set down the bodice piece she was working on and came over to assess the situation. She picked up the failed attempt, turning it over in her hands.

"The issue is the wire." She tapped on the razor-thin metal. "The glove needs a sturdier structure, something that can withstand the heat and weight of the wax without warping."

I rummaged through our supplies. "Let's see, wire, wire, oh, look! More wire. Thread. A condom." I tossed the packet over my shoulder ignoring the muffled laughter of the crew. "Ah-ha!"

I held up a roll of masking tape triumphantly. "This could work."

Mai returned to the dress as I began to wrap the tape around my left hand to create a mold. Layer upon layer of tape wrapped around each finger before I was finally satisfied. Carefully removing the tape—only losing a few hairs in the process—I selected a set of shimmering gold and black candles to go with her dress, adding some super-strength glue to the dripping wax.

Please God, let this work. I don't want to disappoint Mai.

Knowing time was of the essence, I lit every candle, rigging them to drip onto the makeshift glove while I began to make a mold of my left hand.

"This just might work," I murmured as I swapped the first mold out and positioned the remaining candles to cover the second.

Leaving our experiment, I returned to Mai's side, assisting her to tackle the challenge of completing the actual gown.

Precious minutes slipped away as we worked feverishly to add the final flourishes—delicate lace at the hem, glittering crystals cascading down the back, and a last-minute cape made of beautifully soft feathers.

Our model arrived, and Mai helped her into the dress as

I checked our gloves. Holding my breath, I gently peeled the tape away from the wax, praying to whatever God that cared that it would hold.

"Moment of truth," I muttered, breathing a sigh of relief when they held their shape, the wax smooth and unblemished.

"You did it," Mai breathed. "It's stunning."

"Let's see if they'll go on the model."

Slipping each wax glove onto the model's hands took far longer than I had anticipated.

"Hurry," Mai whispered, dancing around me as the clock counted down to zero. "Please!"

Gritting my teeth, I continued to slowly slide them on the model, knowing if I moved too quickly the integrity of the wax might be compromised and our entire design would be wasted.

Sweat trickled down my back, my chest tightening. I had to get this right or Mai's chances were toast.

"Ten seconds!" Michelle called from the stage.

"Theo!" Mai wailed behind me. "Hurry!"

I slid the final glove on, breathing a sigh of relief when the model held up her hands, giving me a nod.

"Tools down!"

I stepped back just as Mai careened into me, wrapping her arms around my middle and throwing me off balance.

I shot a hand out to steady us, laughing at her enthusiasm. "Whoa, babe. Chill. Anyone might think you're warm for my form."

"More than warm," she said, swiping at her eyes. "Look at our design, Theo. It's magnificent."

I had to agree. The dress reminded me of Mai—

understated but not in any way simple. Evocative and powerful, imaginative and clever, it captured the eye and held your interest.

A gown fit-for-royalty, just as the brief demanded. And the gloves, with their glint of gold, added an unexpected edge, a twist of avant-garde flair.

"Not bad," I said, slipping an arm around Mai's waist. "I think we pulled it off."

The judges seemed to agree, praising our innovative use of materials and the cohesive overall look. We were ushered backstage to await the final decision, our hands clasped tightly together.

"I couldn't have done this without you," Mai whispered, leaning her head on my shoulder.

I knew that was a lie, but I appreciated the sentiment.

I pressed a kiss to her hair. "We make a good team—despite you screeching at me to hurry up."

She elbowed me in the side, and I chuckled, pulling her back into me.

And then it was time; the judges filed onto the stage, their faces inscrutable. My heart pounded as they began to speak, detailing the strengths and weaknesses of each look.

"And the first team moving on to the grand finale is...." Erike paused dramatically.

Mai's hand clasped mine tighter, crushing my fingers.

"Jude and Keeley!"

I sagged in my seat, watching as the blonds nodded as if this were their due and not a prize.

They announced Gretchen and Jodie next, leaving only one spot left.

"Mai and Theo," Minerva began sternly. "This look shows immense creativity and skill. However...."

My heart sank. "However" was never a good word coming from the judges. I squeezed Mai's hand as we braced for the blow.

It's okay. I'll help her achieve her dream some other way. No matter how long it takes, Mai is going to have everything her heart desires.

"However," Minerva continued, "we feel that you rose to the occasion and delivered a gown fit for royalty. Congratulations, you're moving on to the grand finale!"

I physically jerked as relief crashed over me like a wave.

"We did it." Letting out a whoop of joy, I turned and wrapped Mai in a fierce hug, capturing her lips with mine. Laughing, I pulled back. "Holy shit, we—"

Mai's hug cut me off. She clung to me like a barnacle, sobbing into my chest.

My mood shifted, turning from joy to warm understanding.

"Baby." I cupped her head, turning my back on the cameras as she hugged me tight. "It's okay. We did it. We're through."

She lifted her head, her tears wet against her cheeks. "I know. It's just—" She sniffed, shuddering. "—I wanted this so bad. So bad, Theo. And now—" She shuddered with another sob.

"Happy tears," I chuckled, swiping at her cheeks. "Happy, happy, happy tears."

She nodded.

We turned back, thanking the judges and commiserating with Dakila and Nina who were eliminated.

"And then there were three," I murmured as we left the warehouse.

Mai nodded, pressing hands to her flushed cheeks. "Tomorrow's the grand finale. We might win."

I chuckled. "Might? Babe, we're going to."

She sighed, leaning against me as the elevator slowly moved up to our floor. "We can only try, right?"

I kissed her head. "Exactly."

"But darn knit all, I want it."

Chuckling, I took her hand, spinning her out of the elevator as the doors opened.

"Then we better get you to bed, Ms. Winner."

"I like the sound of that."

"Hate to interrupt this touching moment," a snide voice said from behind us, "but some of us have to sleep before our big win tomorrow."

I turned to see Jude glaring at us, Keeley at his side.

Mai tensed, her hand tightening in mine. I gave her a reassuring squeeze before releasing her.

"Congratulations on making it through," I said, keeping my tone carefully even. "Guess we'll be seeing more of each other."

Jude rolled his eyes. "That assumes you can keep up."

I met his gaze evenly. "The fact you're bothering us suggests you're intimidated."

Jude scoffed. "Please. You and your little girlfriend got lucky today. But luck won't be enough to win the grand finale. It takes real talent—something you two clearly lack."

I bristled, but I kept my expression neutral. I wasn't about to let this jerk get under my skin. "I guess we'll find out tomorrow," I replied coolly.

"Leave them," Keeley said with a bored sigh. "They're not worthy of our time."

Jude glared at us one last time before he turned on his heel and strutted away, Keeley following close behind.

I watched them, my hands clenching into fists at my sides. "Those arrogant little—"

"Theo." Mai's soft voice broke through my rising anger. "They're not worth it."

I blew out a breath, forcing my muscles to relax.

"You're right," I said, throwing an arm over her shoulder. "Let's get some rest. I want us in peak form to wipe the smirks off their perfectly symmetrical faces once and for all."

Mai giggled. "Stop! That's not nice."

"You can't tell me you didn't notice how perfect their jawlines are."

She snorted. "No, I didn't."

"I guess I must be the one with an eye for lines then."

She chuckled, opening our hotel door. "Your hemming *is* getting better."

"Better? It's perfect. Did you see my line today?"

"Mm, it was as straight as you are," she teased.

"How dare you!"

I crowded her into the room, pressing her against the wall as I shoved the door shut. Nuzzling her neck, I pressed kisses along her sensitive skin.

"Just for that," I said between kisses, "we're going straight to bed."

She groaned, turning her head for a kiss. "Not even one orgasm?"

I wanted to say yes, but Mai deserved someone who put

her needs above their own—even if that need happened to be mine, damn it.

"Nope. Not until we win tomorrow."

She accepted my kiss, melting against me until I pulled back with a rough groan.

"Nope, we're not doing this. Bed, bed, bed!"

She glanced pointedly down at my erection. "He says otherwise."

"He isn't handling needles tomorrow."

She chuckled. "Fair enough." She kicked her shoes off, lining them up next to the door. "You can shower first." She hesitated. "And just to say, I wouldn't be mad if you put on a little show."

"Minx." I wrapped an arm around her, pulling her back into me for a quick kiss. "Tomorrow, after we win."

Later, I lay awake, staring up at the ceiling as I listened to Mai's soft snores.

Winning tomorrow would launch Mai's career to the heights she deserved.

A devil perched on my shoulder. *What happens after her dreams are realized?*

I tightened my arms around her sleeping form protectively, shoving the negative thought away. I'd make sure she got her dream. No matter what it meant for us.

CHAPTER 13
THEO

THEO

Best childhood memory?

MAI

A surprise Disneyland trip. You?

THEO

Eating ice cream with my dog

MAI

Nawww, that's so wholesome

THEO

Should I get a dog?

MAI

Theo...

THEO

Enable me, Mai! Please!

MAI

Go cuddle a kidlet

THEO

> Do you think Annie would let me steal one of the twins? She has two kids, surely, she doesn't need both

MAI

Have you met Annie?

THEO

> I'll buy a dog instead

MAI

Safer bet

We'd assembled early once again, but there was a buzz in the air, a tension of nervous anticipation that hadn't been present during previous rounds.

The director positioned us just so, checking our hair and makeup, and adjusting our clothing.

"Five minutes," Celeste yelled.

I checked the microphone, making sure it was turned off before turning to Mai.

"How you feeling?"

Her fingers twisted the ring on her finger.

"I'm coping."

I caught her around her waist, wrapping her in a hug.

"Before this all goes down I need to say something."

"If it's that I snore—"

I chuckled. "Hush, I'm being serious."

Mai sobered, her gaze searching my face.

"I'm proud of you. You took a chance coming here, and I

know it wasn't easy. You've had a lot of shit thrown at you—not the least by me."

She smiled at that.

"I wanted to thank you for letting me tag along. This has been one of the wildest and best adventures of my life. I know we're going to win because you deserve it, but more importantly, because you're a fucking awesome designer."

"Two minutes!" Celeste yelled, passing by us.

"I want you to know," I continued, "that no matter what happens today, no matter what happens tomorrow, knowing you, being here with you, has been the greatest privilege of my life."

"Oh, Theo." She reached up to pull my head down to kiss me.

"Thank you for everything," she whispered, leaning her forehead against mine. "You've been my rock this whole experience. I couldn't have done it without you."

"Places!" Celeste bellowed, glaring at us.

Reluctantly, we let each other go and turned to the stage as Celeste began the countdown.

"And three, two." She pointed at the cameras.

Michelle stepped onto the stage followed by the three judges.

"Welcome, finalists!" she enthused. "We're into the final round and, baby, do we have a competition for you today!"

She clapped her hands, and out of the wings stepped three models, each wearing different outfits.

"Today we're really putting your talents to the test. Over the next twelve hours, you'll be asked to create three different pieces. A piece will be judged every four hours.

You can present them in any order, but you must present one each time or be disqualified."

She gestured at the models. "Each round you will receive points." She pointed at the back of the stage which lit up with a blank leaderboard. "At the end of the third round, the team with the most points wins!"

She clapped her hands together, grinning. "Are you ready for this?"

Mai shook her head in the negative.

"Great!" Michelle held up a hand. "Ready, steady, sew!"

"Alright, what's our game plan?" I asked, turning to Mai.

She glanced at me, panicked.

"Shit, do you need—"

She held up a hand, halting my question. Taking a deep breath, she closed her eyes and slowly let the breath out of her lungs.

"What's she doing?" I heard one of the crew ask.

"No idea," another responded.

I waited, watching proudly as she conquered her fear and panic, roping in her emotions.

"Accessible fashion," Mai said, opening her eyes. "We're going to create pieces that will help someone."

"Go on," I prompted.

She reached for a drawing pad. "Magnetic closures instead of buttons. A gorgeous suit that's prosthetic friendly. Activewear with easy-access openings and fixtures. A dress that's sexy and comes with a gorgeous built-in leg strap for a wheelchair user."

She began to draw, her pencil flying across the page.

"Accessible by design. That's what we're going for. Fashion that's gorgeous and inclusive."

I grinned, leaning over to watch as her vision began to take shape.

"Add zippers on both sides," I said, tapping on the pants "We want anyone who has a prosthetic to have access—and that might mean they are a double amputee."

"Good point." She added in a quick reference to the zippers.

Her sketches came together as we bounced ideas off each other, incorporating patterns and colors that were unique to us and the brand Mai had created.

"What do you think?" she asked, holding up the drawings for me to see.

I studied the designs carefully, considering not only their form but their intended function. The suit was sleek and modern, with clever magnetic closures in place of fiddly buttons. The activewear featured easy-access zippers, with stylish loops to support one-handed users. And the dress... she'd knocked it out of the park. Flowing and elegant, but perfectly constructed for a wheelchair user to avoid tangling in wheels—not to mention the built-in leg strap, designed for those who needed additional support to hold their legs in place, matched the bodice perfectly.

"Home fucking run," I laughed, lifting my hand for a high five.

She burst out laughing, slapping her hand against mine. "Now the hard part."

I caught her up, cupping her face. "It's only three pieces, Mai. Just remember that. Just three steps stand between you and winning."

I kissed her gently, then pushed her away with a grin, slapping her on the ass. "Let's get to it, Ms. Winner."

I used an iPad to sketch out patterns that would tie each piece together, while Mai went to pull fabrics and fixtures.

The patterns had to be meaningful, something that reflected us.

An idea formed, taking shape.

"Activewear first," she said, pinning an outline to a crimson fabric. "Then the suit, and we'll finish strong with the dress. We need the time to layer it."

"How do you like these?" I asked Mai, showing her the concept.

For the three pieces, I'd pulled together different sketches of *origami* cranes.

"What's the meaning?" Mai asked, tracing her finger over the screen of the iPad.

"This might be cliched, but I feel like these represent us."

I watched as Mai's breath caught. "Paper," she murmured. She glanced up. "That's you."

I nodded.

"And the crane?"

"You told me cranes are symbols of happiness, loyalty and strength." I touched a hand to her hip. "That's you."

She swallowed. "Theo...."

I took the iPad back from her, tapping my finger against the screen. "What do you think? Too corny?"

"Absolutely." She bumped her hip into mine. "I love it. You should hit print."

Breathing out a sigh of relief, I nodded. "Okay. Let's do it."

The hours flew by in a blur of cutting, stitching, and fittings. We moved in tandem, shifting without asking, pivoting when something didn't work, adjusting and cutting, and reworking each and every piece until we were satisfied with the results.

"Time!" Michelle called from the stage. "Designers, submit your first piece."

Our activewear had come together perfectly—a crimson-and-black two-piece that was both stylish, functional, and accessible. We embroidered the origami pattern in the red fabric, subtly adding depth and interest.

I glanced around at the other teams. Gretchen and Jodie had submitted a dynamic yellow-and-black jumpsuit, while Keeley and Jude had created a sleek tulip pant with a braided jacket in an off-cream color.

The judges gushed over the other two teams before coming to us.

I gripped Mai's sweaty hand, offering support.

"Mai and Theo," Michelle announced. "Let's see your first piece."

Mai took a deep breath and stepped forward, our model following her. As she described the adaptable features and inclusive vision behind the activewear, the judges' eyes widened, and I saw them exchange impressed glances.

"This is extraordinary work," Minerva praised. "Combining high fashion with real-world accessibility—I adore your effort. Brava!"

The points were assigned and at the end of round one we were locked in a two-way battle for first with Jude and Keeley.

"Yes," I hissed, shaking Mai back and forth. "We've got this."

We returned to our station, and Mai's hands flew over the machine, a flurry of movement that seemed superhuman. I assisted wherever I could, diligently putting into practice the lessons Mai had taught me.

I stopped for a sip of water, taking a beat to admire my incredible woman. She'd put herself out there, setting her emotions and comfort on fire to do this show. And here she was, bent over her machine, a small crinkle of concentration marring her forehead as she created magic.

I love her.

I twisted the lid back on my water bottle, quietly chuckling to myself.

Of course, I loved her. How could I not fall in love with my best friend? The real revelation was that it had taken me so long to realize. All those dates I'd sabotaged, all those times I'd text her—a basket of fries already ordered. She'd always been the one.

Mine.

"Five minutes remaining!" Michelle called.

"Almost there," Mai murmured, her brow furrowed in concentration as she finished the final seam. She held up the magnetic closure suit jacket, examining it with a critical eye. "What do you think?"

"It's perfect," I assured her. "Stylish, innovative, and made with care for the wearer. The judges will love it."

We sent our model out onto the runway, the navy suit impeccably tailored, the magnetic closures shining subtly as she walked. Mai squeezed my hand nervously as the judges examined the garment.

Alison ran an approving hand over the fabric. "Excellent construction and such a clever, inclusive design. Your choice of the shape of the magnetic closures is perfect —it looks luxe while still being functional. And I must say, I love how you've once again used pattern to tie the pieces together. Well done."

Gretchen and Jodie clawed back some points with a denim one-piece made from vintage scraps sewn into a patchwork quilt-like pattern. Jude and Keeley, meanwhile, produced a rather sensual piece of lingerie in a dark green that the judges had loved.

Despite Gretchen and Jodie's hard work, the points once again had us neck and neck with Jude and Keeley going into the final round.

"We're taking a lunch break," Michelle announced. "Please help yourself to food."

We headed over to the catering table and loaded up our plates. Gretchen and Jodie took a seat beside us, both looking glum.

"We're too far behind," Gretchen said, poking at her sandwich. "We'll never make up the points."

"Don't be like that." Mai bumped her with her shoulder. "Anything could happen. We could rip the train off a dress at the last minute—"

"Done that," I said around a mouth full of food.

"Or cut your hand open and bleed on the satin."

I held up my bandaged pinky finger. "Guilty."

"Or—"

Gretchen laughed, shaking her head. "Okay, okay, I get it. We could have a miracle."

"You could," Mai said firmly. "And that's exciting."

I couldn't help but notice Jude and Keeley glaring daggers at us from across the room. I ignored them, taking a huge bite out of my sandwich.

So much for not being worthy of your time.

As lunch finished, I excused myself, heading for the bathroom. I was washing my hands when Jude entered.

He stopped beside me, crossing his arms, his glare still in place.

"You know," I said easily, pulling a paper towel from the dispenser. "You'll get more wrinkles if you keep frowning like that."

"You're about to lose."

I snorted, tossing the used paper in the recycling. "Hate to break it to you, buddy, but we're tied. This is anyone's game."

"That's what you think."

I narrowed my eyes at him. "You know something I don't? 'Cause so far the judges have been pretty clear about their opinions."

Jude smirked, an ugly expression for such a beautiful man. "I know your little secret. You lied. Your relationship is a sham. And tonight, everyone else is going to know it too."

The breath caught in my chest, and I had to work to keep my tone even. "Bullshit. Mai and I are the real deal."

"Is that so?" He pulled his phone from his pocket and held it out to me. There in technicolor were texts I'd exchanged with a woman I'd tried dating about six months ago. She'd been nice, but we didn't have any chemistry. We'd met for one date before agreeing there wasn't anything to pursue.

Because you'd been in love with Mai.

"Either you're a cheater, or you're lying. Which is it?"

I swallowed. "How do you know these aren't fake?"

He chuckled. "This woman happens to be my cousin. I know you met up for a date—she recognized you from the promotions."

Fuck.

"So?" I said with a shrug. "Mai and I were on a break. We worked it out."

"You really think people will believe that?" He chuckled, sliding the phone into his pocket. "I know the editor of the *Astipia Daily*. Once these are out in the open, I own the narrative." He leaned in, his expression a smirking mess of nasty. "And how many others will come forward?"

None since his cousin, but there'd been more before her.

I'd overlooked my dating history when convincing Mai to join the show, too focused on wanting to give her this opportunity to recognize that I needed to protect her from my past. But that didn't matter now. All the matter was that Mai and I were real.

I made a dismissive gesture, begrudgingly amused by Jude's threat. "So go ahead. Mai and I will tell the truth. It's not a big deal."

"No?" Jude inclined his head toward the bathroom door. "Your *girlfriend* fell apart when they handed her candles. You really think she's going to cope when your relationship is dissected on every national morning show?"

I sobered as the implication hit me, squeezing my chest and turning my blood to ice.

I could blow this off and work with the network to

brazen our way through it—but I'd seen how gossip ripped people apart. Even a whiff of scandal resulted in people's lives being destroyed as they were dragged through the mud.

I refused to allow that to happen to Mai.

I searched Jude's face, trying to understand his motivation. "Is this about me? Or are you scared she's going to beat you?"

Jude's gaze flicked away, the only concession to my accusation.

"What do you want?" I ground out.

"For you to lose."

"Why?"

"I've read up on you. What have you achieved? Nothing. You've ridden on the coattails of your brother for more than a decade." His humorless chuckle crackled down my spine. "No one expects you to win. You're a barely functioning human being."

His comments landed a minor blow, but I brushed them off. "We got to the final, didn't we?"

"*She* did. You're just lucky the other teams performed poorly."

He turned away to wash his hands. Pity the water couldn't wash away his spite.

I clenched my jaw, fighting for calm. "What exactly are you asking?"

Jude didn't even spare me a glance. "Throw the game. Unless you have two-hundred and fifty thousand lying around to pay me to silence the story?"

I ground my teeth together, remaining silent.

"I didn't think so." He turned the tap off and reached for a paper towel.

"You're broke."

Jude slowly crumpled up the towel, tossing it in a nearby trashcan.

"That isn't relevant."

"This is blackmail."

He arched an eyebrow. "Can you prove it?"

"What happens if I do what you ask?" I asked, my lips numb. Impotent rage burned in my gut, my hands shaking from the injustice.

He shrugged. "These images stay between us."

"And if I don't?"

He chuckled. "You know what will happen."

Mai.

Fear hit me like a ton of bricks, clawing at my chest. "I can't throw the competition. She's worked too hard for this."

"Then don't be surprised when these are published." He walked away, then paused in the bathroom doorway, glancing back. "I predict you'll both be ruined."

With that parting shot, he left, leaving me to death grip the bathroom sink. I lifted my head, staring at the man in the mirror.

"Shit," I muttered. "What the fuck do I do?"

My reflection didn't answer.

CHAPTER 14
MAI

Something was wrong with Theo.

He'd returned from the bathroom pale and drawn, his jaw ticking.

"Everything okay?" I asked quietly as the show runners set up for the next take.

"Fine," he said tersely, not meeting my eyes.

I frowned but didn't push, knowing he'd tell me in his own time. I reached over to give his hand a reassuring squeeze, but he pulled away, tucking his hands into his pockets, acting like he hadn't seen me moving toward him.

His rejection felt like a slap. Hurt and confused, I opened my mouth to call him on it, but Michelle interrupted.

"You time restarts, now!"

I bit my lip, glancing at the clock. We had four hours left in the competition—precious few minutes so I couldn't dedicate time to whatever was going on with him.

Shoving my concerns aside, I pointed at the fabric still to be pinned. "Can you do that?"

He nodded tightly, still not meeting my gaze.

I began cutting and pinning the bodice, hand stitching the delicate material while Theo worked on the skirt.

But with every passing minute, my anxiety mounted. Theo's deft fingers fumbled with the delicate material, ripping the thin lace. His seams were crooked, and his hems half finished. At one point, he knocked over a tray of sequins, sending them scattering across the floor.

"Leave it," I said when he bent to clean them up. "We don't have time."

He just shook his head, scooping handfuls back into the tray with shaking hands. Across the room, I caught Jude smirking at us. Unease slithered down my spine.

"Two hours remaining!" Michelle called.

My eyes widened in horror as I took in the state of our dress. It was a disaster—puckered seams, gaps in the beading, hemline uneven. Tears of frustration pricked my eyes.

"Theo," I said, fighting to keep my voice calm. "I need

you to either tell me what's wrong or pull it together. Please. This is too important."

His haunted green eyes met mine. I searched his gaze, struggling to understand what had happened.

"How can I help?" I asked, laying a hand on his arm. "Tell me."

As we stared at each other, his vacant, hopeless look disappeared, replaced by something like determined resignation.

"Fuck you're brave." He gestured at the cameras around us. "You don't even care that they're watching me melt down."

"I care. I just do it anyway."

"Fuck." He pulled me close, holding me tight. "You're right. This *is* too important."

He let me go and turned to the mannequin, tugging the skirt free. Wadding it up, he tossed the material onto our workbench.

"Let's get to work."

Relieved to have him back, we found our rhythm once more. Our movements were synchronized, a seamless dance of fabric and thread.

"That's it," Theo said, passing me a perfectly presented skirt. "We're nearly done."

I draped the fabric, cutting and basting with efficiency as he tucked and stitched the final pieces.

Our dress took shape, transforming into its intended vision. The once-gaping holes were closed, the puckered seams smoothed, and the uneven hemline corrected. Imperfections were hidden by clever layering and strategically placed embellishments.

"Time's up!" Michelle called, clapping her hands. "Congratulations, contestants! You're done."

I sagged to the floor, laughing as the reality of what we'd achieved hit me.

"We did it," I breathed, tilting my head back to stare up at Theo. "We finished."

My back and neck ached, and my fingers were half-numb from overuse. But we'd done it. And no one could take this away from us.

Theo returned my smile, a flicker of his old humor returning. "You better believe it."

I pushed up from the floor, hesitantly reaching out for a hug. This time he didn't pull away. He hauled me into his arms, holding me tight.

"I'm sorry," he muttered against my hair.

"It's okay." I clung to the warmth and security of his embrace. "Are you okay?"

He remained silent for a long time. "No. I let Jude get to me, and I almost ruined everything for you." He squeezed me tighter, and I could feel him trembling slightly. "I'm sorry, Mai. I underestimated you."

"Jude? What do you mean?" I asked, pulling back to look him in the eye.

He hesitated. "It's—let's talk about this later. Tonight is about you."

I frowned. "But, Theo, what—"

"Later. I promise."

Fear gnawed at my insides, a thousand scenarios running through my head at breakneck speed. I wanted to press him, to demand he tell me. But cameras circled the room, catching our every move.

"Later," I agreed reluctantly. "But I'm holding you to that."

The judges examined our final design, picking over every blemish, missed stitch, and pulled thread.

The judges circled our final design, their critical eyes taking in every detail. I held my breath, my heart pounding as they examined the dress from every angle.

Erike lifted the hem, inspecting the stitching. "The construction here is impeccable, especially given the time constraints." He slid a meaningful glance at Theo. "And you've managed to disguise any imperfections with layering and embellishments. I'm begrudgingly impressed."

Theo tipped his head at Erike. "I'll take that."

Alison ran a hand along the bodice of the gown. "I love the way you've incorporated the leg strap into the overall design and echoed the details of the bodice. It's functional and fashionable, without compromising on either aspect."

I felt almost giddy as Minerva stepped back, taking in the full effect of the dress.

"It's a stunning piece, and unique. We don't see many accessible by design pieces," she said, walking around the model. "The way you've tied together the crane motifs across all three designs is a testament to your creativity and cohesion as a team."

I felt Theo's hand find mine, our fingers intertwining. We exchanged a glance, a mixture of relief, pride, and anticipation passing between us.

"Well done," Michelle whispered as the judges moved on. "High praise indeed."

The set became a flurry of motion as the crew set up for the final announcement.

"No matter what happens," Theo whispered, squeezing my hand, "I'm proud of you, Mai. You've poured your heart and soul into this competition, and it shows in every stitch, every seam, every design."

I leaned into him, drawing on his strength. "I couldn't have done it without you." I mean every word. When I'd felt overwhelmed by emotion, he'd given me a safe place to land. It was through him that I'd discovered a confidence in myself and my ability to handle the unknown.

"All right people, places!" Celeste called, clapping her hands.

The cameras began to roll, and I twisted my ring over and over as the judges deliberated on stage. We awaited their verdict, my chest a bundle of writhing nerve endings.

With a final nod, they turned to the contestants, their expressions solemn.

"Jodie and Gretchen," Michelle began, smiling. "You stayed true to your brand, creating pieces as magnificent and bold as they are functional. It has been a pleasure to see your efforts throughout this competition, and watch the two of you sparkle together."

She turned. "Jude and Keeley, your designs are a reflection of your commitment to quality. The construction of your garments are second to none—and I believe you've even managed to step outside your comfort zone and create pieces that challenged even your high standards."

Keeley clasped her hands in front of her chest and bowed slightly in thanks.

"Mai and Theo," Michelle said, her voice cutting through the tension. "Your designs throughout this competition have been nothing short of remarkable. You've consistently pushed the boundaries of fashion while prioritizing inclusivity. Tonight, you've shown us that true innovation comes from the heart and accessibility in fashion can be both functional and beautiful."

She stepped back, gesturing at Erike to step forward.

"The scores have been tallied, and we have our winners. But before we reveal the results, I want to say that each and every one of you should be proud of what you've accomplished here. You've shown the world that fashion is for everyone, and that true beauty comes in all forms." He pulled an envelope from his back pocket.

"The judges have made our decision," Erike declared. "And the winners of this year's *Perfect Fit* are...." He paused for dramatic effect.

I held my breath, my heart pounding in my ears. This was it, the moment of truth. We'd fought so hard to be here, worked ourselves to the bone to make this happen. As if hearing my thoughts, Theo pulled me into him, wrapping an arm around my shoulders to squeeze me tight.

"Jude and Keeley!"

I sagged, the excitement and anticipation leaving my body in a rush. Exhaustion hit me with an almost-overwhelming thump.

Tears clogged the back of my throat even as I smiled through the pain.

It had always been a long shot. But I'd hoped.

Theo and I clapped politely, smiling and nodding as Jude and Keeley accepted their award.

"But the night isn't over," Erike said, waggling his finger.

"While the prize money has been won, a second prize is still to be awarded."

I exchanged a look with Theo, mouthing silently, "Second prize?"

"Tonight, I will be offering the designer who I believe shows the most promise an exclusive experience. For the next four weeks you will intern with me as we work to create your first runway show for Milan Fashion Week."

My mouth dropped open, my heart pounding in my chest.

"You might have wondered why you signed on for six weeks when the competition is already complete." He grinned. "The cameras will follow you over the next four weeks as you develop your designs and work around the clock to ready them. They will be there to capture your triumph as you debut your first show."

His gaze locked with mine. "Mai, I would like to invite you to join me."

My mind blanked. Sound disappeared, and I looked at Erike as if he were at the other end of a long tunnel.

Is this happening? Did he really just say my name?

Theo's roar shook me from my shock.

"Mai! You're going to Italy!" He wrapped me in a bear hug, lifting me up.

"Theo!" I squealed, thumping against his shoulders. "You'll hurt yourself!"

"Psh!" he scoffed. "You did it, Mai. You fucking won!"

The show wrapped up and Erike came over to congratulate me.

"To be clear," he told Theo, shaking his hand, "this offer is for Mai only."

I stiffened, my stomach dropping.

"Of course," Theo said easily. "Mai's the one who deserves this."

Erike congratulated me once more, reminding me that I'd need to be at the airport by five in the morning before he moved away.

Turning to Theo, I clasped my shaking hands together, desperately trying to hold my sudden panic at bay.

"Theo, I can't—you—I need—"

He clasped his hands on my shoulders, dipping down to stare into my eyes.

"You can. And, Mai, you have to. I can't come with you to do this. God knows I would if I could, but I can't."

"I'll cancel," I said, running through my options. "Or maybe we could—"

He cut me off with a shake of his head. "No, baby. This is one path I can't walk with you—and it's one path that I know you have to take. You'll hate yourself if you don't."

I hated that he knew that. I hated that I wanted him to tell me all was okay. Hated that I needed him to help me through this.

I wasn't strong enough to do this by myself.

"I can't."

"Yes, you fucking can." He tapped my nose with his finger. "You're Mai fucking Sakamoto. You are brave, you are talented, and you're going to slay on that runway."

I needed him.

"Theo, take me to bed."

His eyebrows rose. "You're sure?"

I nodded. "I need you to make love to me."

He hesitated for a brief beat, then cursed softly. "Fuck

it." He yanked his microphone out of his shirt, tossing it at the nearest assistant.

"Let's go."

CHAPTER 15
MAI

The bed sank under my weight, creaking softly as I watched Theo undress.

Our gazes were locked as he slowly peeled off his shirt, revealing broad shoulders and a firm chest.

A chest I desperately wanted to kiss.

He stripped off his pants and sat by the bed, slowly

removing his prosthetic. I reached for the buttons on my dress but Theo stopped me.

"No," he whispered, placing a hand on my ankle. "Let me."

He crawled up the bed to settle next to me, his hands gentle as he unbuttoned my shirt, revealing my skin. I watched his fingers trace delicate circles on my stomach, caressing up my torso to unclip my bra in one smooth move.

"Well done," I said, my voice choked.

"If that impressed you, wait until you see my next trick."

He leaned down to blow warm air against my nipples, hardening them into peaks. I shivered as his lips grazed my breast, his tongue swirling delicately before drawing my nipple into his warm mouth. Sparks of pleasure spread like wildfire as his hand slid down to push down my skirt.

I lay bare before him, heart pounding, as his eyes raked over my body hungrily.

"You're so beautiful, Mai," he murmured, fingers trailing up my inner thigh. I shivered at his touch.

He settled between my legs, pressing hot, open-mouthed kisses along my stomach and hip bones. I threaded my fingers through his hair as his mouth moved lower, teasing me with featherlight touches. A moan escaped my lips.

"Theo, please...." I whimpered, arching toward him. He obliged, tongue delving into my slick folds. Pleasure crashed over me as he licked and sucked, stoking the fire within me higher and higher. My thighs trembled as he drove me to the edge. With a few skillful flicks of his tongue, I shattered, crying out his name.

"See." He grinned up at me. "Told you, you'd be impressed."

Groaning, I shoved his head back down to my clit. "Shut up and worship me."

He made a growling sound of affirmation, renewing his attention.

I writhed against the sheets, my fingers yanking at his hair as the tension inside me coiled tighter and tighter. Just as I was about to climax again, he pulled back, his hot breath teasing my sensitive flesh.

"You taste incredible," he murmured huskily, pressing a soft kiss to my inner thigh. "I could do this all night."

I whimpered, trying to push his face back where I needed it most. "Don't you dare stop. Don't you dare!"

Chuckling, he dipped his head and worked me with a few deliberate strokes. Within a beat, I began shaking with the force of my climax.

I tugged at his hair, begging him wordlessly to climb up my body.

"Fuck, condom."

In a fumble of hands, I hauled the complimentary goodies box out of the bedside drawer and shoved it at him.

"Hurry!"

He pulled one of the condoms out of the box, seeming to take great delight in examining the packaging.

"Theo!"

"What?" he asked cheekily. "Just checking if it's ribbed for your pleasure."

"If you don't get that thing on now, so help me God, I'll—"

Chuckling, he ripped the foil open with his teeth and rolled the latex on in one smooth move.

"Wrap your legs around me." He settled over me, his weight deliciously heavy.

Wrapping my legs around his waist, I pulled him closer, desperate to be filled by him, surrounded by him. He reached down to line himself up, the blunt head of his erection nudging my entrance. With a swift thrust of his hips, Theo buried himself inside me.

We both groaned at the exquisite pressure. Theo set a steady rhythm, driving into me with deep, powerful strokes. I clung to his shoulders, meeting each thrust eagerly. The room filled with the sounds of our ragged breathing and the slap of flesh against flesh.

I clung to him as he drove into me again and again, adjusting his angle until he found the perfect spot.

"Theo," I panted, "I'm so close."

"Me too," he grunted. "Come for me, Mai. Let go."

His hand snaked between our bodies, playing with my clit.

With a cry, I shattered as waves of ecstasy crashed over me. Theo followed me over the edge with a hoarse shout, his hips stuttering against mine as he found his release.

We collapsed together on the bed, breathing hard, bodies slick with sweat.

"That was...." I trailed off, unable to find adequate words.

"Amazing? Earth-shattering? The best sex of your life?" he offered breathlessly.

"Wow, such humility."

He chuckled, then groaned. "Fuck. Why did we wait this long?"

"Ignorance," I said, feeling dazed. "We didn't know what we were missing."

"Never again," he said. Theo rolled until he could catch my lips in a kiss.

"Never," I agreed, tangling my fingers in his hair.

We kissed, slowly, then with building passion.

"Again?" I panted.

"Abso-fucking-lutely."

CHAPTER 16

MAI

A tear slipped free as Theo moved inside me. The alarm clock by the bed glowed in harsh red digits, 3:48 a.m., a stark reminder of the rapidly dwindling time we had left together.

"Come with me," I whispered, needing him.

I hated how the inevitability of our separation hung

heavy in the air, infusing each touch, each kiss, each whispered word with a bittersweet intensity.

Theo's hands roamed my body with reverent hunger, his fingertips tracing the contours of my curves. I kept my eyes open, committing every touch, every groan, every shiver to memory. I clung to him, my nails raking down his back, desperate to imprint the feel of his skin against mine, to etch this moment indelibly into my being.

We moved as one, our bodies entwined. Each powerful thrust of his hips, each sensual roll of mine, built the desire between us. Despite the ticking of the clock, we didn't rush, desperate to draw every second out.

As the dawn began to creep through the windows, painting the walls, Theo's kisses changed. They became desperate, hungry, rough.

I met him stroke for stroke, our rhythm building to a crescendo, the unspoken depths of our feelings pouring through our physical connection.

I love you.

The words hovered between us, unspoken, unacknowledged. I wanted to taste them on his lips, whisper them in his ears, write them onto his heart.

He gathered me close, his lips trailing worshipful kisses along my hairline, my temple, my jaw, before claiming my mouth in a kiss that left me breathless and aching.

"Now," he murmured, nipping at my lip. "Come for me, Mai."

His hand slipped between us, his fingers sliding across my clit as he adjusted his angle. He moved me, finding new depth, a new tempo, a new way to drive me wild.

I clawed at Theo's back, my head falling to the bed as I

arched up, pressing my hips to his as he fucked me, made love to me, rode me into oblivion.

I came, clutching around his cock as I heard his shout, his thrusts growing uneven as he followed me over.

We collapsed together, our limbs intertwined as we gasped for air, both of us carefully avoiding the clock.

But the real world intruded with the incessant beeping of the alarm.

Theo reached out, slapping the alarm clock as he pulled me close, kissing my head.

"I don't want to go," I admitted in a whisper. "Don't make me."

He sighed, running hands over my back in soothing, slow strokes. "You have to, Mai. It's only for four weeks. It's too good an opportunity to pass up."

"Can't you come? Please?"

He cupped my cheeks in his hands. "You can do this, Mai. I know you think you need me, but you don't. I promise. It's going to be scary. It's going to be hard. But I'll be a phone call away if you need me." He let go of my cheeks to catch my hand, pulling it to his lips. "When you're lonely, think of this."

He kissed my ring—the ring he'd given me.

I closed my eyes, forcing myself to be brave, to be strong, to be the woman he saw in me.

"I can do this."

"Yeah, you can."

I swallowed, fighting back the fear. "I'm doing this."

His fingers brushed stray dark strands of my hair from my cheek. "And I'll be cheering you on the whole time."

I relaxed against him, placing my ear over his heart. "What will you do for the next four weeks?"

He sighed. "I...."

I lifted my head. "Theo?"

He shook his head. "I need to have a conversation with Linc."

"About?"

"Leaving the company."

I stiffened. "I thought you loved it there?"

He sighed again, raising a hand to pinch the bridge of his nose. "The timing of this conversation is shit. We have to get you to the airport."

"Then give me the abridged version while I pack."

I waited until he gave a sharp nod.

I rolled out of bed and pulled on a robe, beginning to pack as I waited for him to start.

Theo shuffled up the bed, shoving a pillow behind him so he could lean against the wooden headboard.

"I've realized that the only reason I stuck around was because I thought Linc needed me. And in the beginning when the whole place was falling down around his ears, he did. But now...." Theo raised his hands in a half shrug. "I'm superfluous."

"I don't think that's true, but I understand the sentiment." I folded my things into my suitcase, quietly considering his confession. "What would you like to do with your life?"

He shrugged. "No idea. But seeing you find your passion and pursue it—it's inspiring as fuck, Mai. I've envied you these last few weeks. I want what you have."

"High anxiety?" I asked, only half-joking.

"Passion. Drive. Determination. Commitment. Fuck." He slumped on the bed. "I sound like a real catch right about now."

I tossed a sock into my bag and crawled up the bed to settle beside him.

"You know, there's a lot of power in not knowing what you want to be when you grow up," I said lightly. "The world is your oyster. You can sample and choose whatever you want to do. That's exciting."

He chuckled, shooting me a look. "I guess that's one way to look at it. Do you happen to know anyone looking for an intern?"

I leaned over, kissing the tip of his nose. "Consider this your challenge."

"What? Unemployment?"

I shook my head. "Finding your purpose."

"Would it be corny if I said my purpose is you?"

I snorted. "Yes."

He ran knuckles over the curve of my cheek. "Not to mention unfair to turn you into my entire life. It gives off a whiff of stalker."

"I prefer to see myself as a cult leader." I pulled the sash free from my robe, grinning as his gaze dropped to my breasts. "Worship me."

His hands came up just as there was a thumping knock at the door.

"Not a-fucking-gain," Theo growled, dropping his hands. "What?" he called, sounding surly as fuck.

"It's Bruce. Taxi leaves in five minutes!"

"Fuck!" I squeaked, springing out of bed. "Fuck, fuck, fuck!"

"You get dressed, I'll pack," Theo ordered, reaching for his crutch. "Hurry, babe."

I raced around the hotel room, tugging on whatever was closest to hand as I attempted to both brush my teeth and run a comb through my hair at the same time.

I exited the bathroom, tossing my toiletries bag to Theo who caught it and plunked it in my suitcase. He'd somehow managed to pack all my stuff, set out my shoes and socks, and pull on some pants in the same short time I'd had to freak out.

Zipping up my suitcase, he leaned heavily on his crutch as he moved across the room. He opened the door to the hotel room, gesturing at Bruce to come in.

"Take this downstairs," he ordered, pointing at the suitcase. "Mai needs a minute."

Bruce glanced pointedly at his watch. "We need to leave in—"

"Just take it down. She'll be there."

Sniffing, Bruce did as told, leaving us alone.

Finished with my laces, I stood, accepting my backpack from Theo. I tugged it on, search his face.

"Are we okay?"

Without hesitating, his free arm shot out, fisting my shirt and hauling me across the short distance between us. His lips caught mine, possessing me with hungry, delicious desire.

I returned his kiss, mindful of his crutch and balance.

"Never, ever doubt my feelings for you," he grunted between kisses.

Breathing heavily, I stepped back, brushing at a stray tear. "I'll see you in four weeks."

Theo glanced over his shoulder at the clock on the bedside table.

"Twenty-seven days, eighteen hours, and thirty-nine minutes," he agreed.

I sucked in a deep breath, twirling the ring on my finger. "Text me?"

"I will."

He leaned over, kissing me one final time. "Enjoy it, Mai. You've earned it."

"And you." I waggled my finger in his face. "Go find your passion."

With a parting, lingering glance, I opened the door and left.

It only took until the taxi left the hotel driveway for my courage to flee.

"What am I doing?" I asked, feeling my anxiety rise.

"Going to the airport?" Bruce said from his spot in the front. He glanced back at me, his eyebrow raised. "Are you hung over or something?"

I shook my head, turning away to stare out the window of the taxi, fighting for breath.

My phone vibrated in my pocket and I tugged it out, welcoming the distraction.

THEO

By now you'll have started panicking. Don't. You're brave, Mai. You're a lion, a tiger, a fucking bear. You are a warrior and a worrier—and both serve you well. But don't let the worrier win when courage should triumph

I closed my eyes, centering myself.

I could do this.

I can do this.

I am doing this.

By the time we reached the airport I felt—if not less anxious at least a manageable level of anxiety.

"Oh," I heard behind me as I stepped from the taxi. "It's you."

I glanced up to see Celeste exiting a limo, a coffee cup in hand.

"Celeste, hey." I gestured at the airport. "Are you going to Milan as well?"

"Of course. This is my show, I'll be there for the first week of filming before handing it over to my assistant director."

"Ah." I accepted my suitcase from Bruce and followed her into the terminal. "Did you want to get a muffin or something?"

She scoffed. "With my frequent flyer miles? I'm off to a lounge."

I tried not to smile at Bruce's disappointed expression. "Of course."

She glanced at me as we walked. "I hear your boyfriend is flying home today. A pity, he's quite good on TV."

I huffed out a laugh. "Yeah, he's definitely the more entertaining of the two of us."

"I've never seen one person fuck up so badly—and yet you saved his ass time and time again. I lost a decent chunk betting you'd be out by the second round. It'll make for great ratings." We reached the terminal, slipping through security quickly.

"We're this way," Bruce said, pointing toward the gate. "Celeste is on a later flight."

"Well, it was good to see you," I said awkwardly to her. "Have a good flight."

"Yes," she answered, distracted by her phone.

I watched her walk off, something niggling at the back of my mind as she side stepped a group of air-hostesses.

They walked past me, and I heard one of them say, "...first day. It's going to be hilarious. You'll get everything wrong, but don't worry. It's only up from here."

An idea smacked into me, snapping into my consciousness like a jolt of lightning.

"Celeste, wait!"

She turned, brow arched as I ran toward her, skidding to a stop in the terminal.

She glanced at her watch. "You have five minutes."

"You said you found Theo floundering on *Perfect Fit* funny, right?"

"Honey, the man's a complete himbo, fucking acting like he had some skills. I saw through you both on day one." She shook her head. "I have no idea how you did it, but you somehow taught him how to not be completely useless in the process." She chuckled.

I ignored her less that flattering assessment of Theo in favor of the bigger picture.

"What would you say to watching him do that again?"

Celeste shifted, transferring her coffee from one hand to the other. "Go on."

"You could do a series where Theo tries different jobs from around the country. He's great with people, charismatic, and you said he's good in front of the camera."

Her fingers clicked against her coffee cup as she considered my pitch. "What do I get out of this?"

"My everlasting devotion?"

"Try again."

I searched around, trying to find the right incentive.

"You said yourself he's hilarious. And you have to admit he'd be a great moneymaker. The audience will love watching him rise to the challenges."

And I knew he'd love trying new things and meeting people. If he happened to find his calling along the way, so much the better.

I mentally crossed all my fingers and toes, praying she'd say yes.

"Hmm." Her fingers stopped clicking. "Let me run this up the line. I'll call you."

"You like it?" I asked, delighted.

"I didn't say that." She made a tutting sound. "Don't run after me at airports ever again. I like my anonymity."

With that brisk comment, she turned on her heel and strode down the concourse toward her gate, leaving me to stare after her.

"Well, darn knit all," I muttered, grinning. "She liked the idea."

I reached for my phone but hesitated. I didn't want to get Theo's hopes up. I decided to wait until after I'd heard from Celeste. It would either be good news, or a funny story of how badly I pitched a TV show.

"Mai!" Bruce hollered from down the terminal. "We're boarding!"

Turning, I raced to my gate, praying all would work out.

CHAPTER 17
THEO

MAI

I miss you

THEO

I miss you too

MAI

What have you been up to?

THEO

Missing you

MAI

And?

THEO

Jerking off to thoughts of you

MAI

THEO!

THEO

What? You want me to sweet-talk you? I stroketh mine throbbing member to the memory of thy taste on my lips. I burn for you, my sweet kumquat

MAI

I hate that I laughed

I t had been thirteen days, three hours and eighteen minutes since I'd hugged Mai for the last time before she'd boarded the plane for Milan. I found myself regularly daydreaming about seeing her, touching her, tasting her.

A basketball hit me in the face, jerking me back to reality.

"Shit! Sorry, man!" Jay Wood ran across the court to lay a hand on my shoulder. "You okay?"

I rubbed my nose, nodding. "That's what I get for zoning out."

Upon my return to the Cove, our weekly basketball ritual had recommenced—Linc, Jay, Ren, and I duking it out on the local court. Winner took all—while the losers had to pay for the first round of drinks.

Jay searched my face. "Your nose might be fine but something else is chewing at you."

I huffed out a laugh, shoving him away. "How about you leave the mental health diagnosis to your wife."

"It's about Mai, right?"

My head whipped to stare at Ren who stood behind me, his hands on his hips.

"You've been a morose bastard since you got back." His lips quirked at one side. "You fell in love with her."

I opened my mouth to deny then sighed. "Yeah, I did. Hard."

"I fucking knew it." Linc shoved me. "Why didn't you say anything?"

"I haven't told her yet." I scrubbed a hand over my still smarting face. "Not to mention the whole Italy thing."

"What about Italy?" Jay asked, absently spinning the ball on one finger.

I glanced around the empty indoor court—the faded bleachers and fluorescent lighting were as familiar to me as my own hand. Our weekly games—when we were all in town—were more than just four guys shooting the shit. They'd become an outlet for us, a place to share our struggles.

I pointed at Ren. "You going to get weird that I'm talking about your sister?"

"Not unless you're saying something derogatory." He crossed his arms over his chest. "But I'll give you a warning before I start punching."

"Fair." I sighed, stepping back to flop onto the worn wooden bleacher behind me. "I'm a fuck-up."

Linc and Ren dropped on either side of me while Jay chose to sit on the basketball, rolling gently back and forth.

"Explain," Jay said, and I appreciated that he didn't deny my statement.

"I want...."

Fuck. How did one describe this aching need inside them? It went beyond missing Mai, beyond the love I had for her, to some long-forgotten part of who I was.

"I want," I said again with a sigh. "I want her to have everything she desires—be it a fashion house in Milan, world travel, babies—whatever she wants."

"That's about her. What—beyond my sister—do you want?" Ren prompted.

"The fuck if I know." I sighed, leaning back in my seat to stare up at the scuff-marked ceiling.

"This is probably not the time to do this," Linc said, drawing my gaze to him. "But Annie and I have talked, and we both agree—I'm sorry, bro. But we need to fire you."

I jerked upright. "The fuck, dude?"

"Oh, harsh," Jay said with a wince.

Linc's green gaze met my own, his expression sympathetic but determined. "Let's be honest, you're not happy at the company." He held up a hand to halt my protests. "You're not, Theo. You haven't been for a long time, and I've been too selfish to recognize it. You deserve to leave and find your true passion."

I swallowed, feeling a weight shift off my shoulders. "What about the business?"

"We're good. Promise. While you were away, the team stepped up. They did a stellar job." He placed a hand on my shoulder. "You know you'll always have a place here. But it's time for you to work out what you want. And I refuse to be the fucker who holds you back."

I blew out a breath. "Well, fuck. You've stolen my thunder."

He cocked an eyebrow.

"I've been trying to think of a way to quit for the past two weeks. I love you, don't get me wrong. But coming back here—it doesn't fit anymore." I shook my head. "I don't know what I want to do or where I want to be—but I know I want to do it with Mai."

Ren huffed and I turned to him.

"I'm happy for you." He shook his head. "But if you knit me anything for Christmas, I will revoke my approval."

"You can knit me a body condom," Jay said with a laugh. "These ungrateful dicks don't appreciate true workmanship."

I reached down and pulled out a hundred-dollar note from my sock and handed it to Ren.

"What's this?" he asked, accepting it with two fingers and a wrinkled nose.

"For losing the bet."

He frowned for a second then laughed. "So no quickie wedding?"

"Not this year." I blew out my breath. "When I marry your sister, it'll be because we're ready. Not because of some bet."

"When? Awfully presumptuous of you."

I grinned, not denying it.

"So, what are you going to do now?" Jay asked, rocking on the ball. "Run for city council? Raise goats? Learn a new trade?"

"Fuck if I know." I shrugged. "Guess I'll have to figure it out."

Linc clapped a hand on my shoulder as he pushed himself to a stand. "I'll be magnanimous and allow you to keep your job until you work out your next step—but don't get comfy. There's a time limit on your employment."

I chuckled, allowing him to haul me up. "Yes, boss."

He pulled me in for a quick, back-slapping hug. "I'm proud of you, Theo. Change is never easy."

"Tell me about it."

Jay followed us back onto the court, tossing the ball back and forth with Ren.

"It's a pity you can't go try a bunch of different jobs to find one that fits."

Ren snorted. "Can you imagine? I'd pay good money to watch Theo trying to teach kindergarteners their numbers."

"Or hauling fish—the guy would fall overboard in the first five minutes."

Linc snorted. "Overboard? He gets seasick."

"Once! I got seasick once!"

Jay wrapped an arm around my shoulders, squeezing. "It's okay. You can come learn how to work wood with me."

"Fuck no!" Ren shuddered. "Do you want him to cut all his fingers off?"

"I hate you all," I told them, intercepting the ball. "Now let's play."

That night I lay in bed staring up at the ceiling and wishing I could text Mai but our time zone difference meant she'd be sleeping soundly.

My conversation with the guys played through my head over and over.

I knew what I wanted—Mai. But a job that fulfilled me would be nice too.

I glanced at my clock. Fourteen days, one hour and three minutes down. Which meant there was still a lifetime to go until her internship ended.

I lifted my phone, turned on the bedside lamp, and snapped off a picture of me cuddling with Urma.

THEO

We miss you

Knowing she'd laugh when she woke, I clicked off the light and closed my eyes, silently counting the minutes until I'd see her again.

CHAPTER 18
MAI

I ached in both body and soul. I'd worked my way through missing Theo by throwing myself into the work required to pull together my first fashion show, but today the ache wouldn't end.

Erike paused at my table, frowning as he checked my work.

His studio was a dream come true, and being tutored by a master, it fulfilled my greatest wish.

"This is good," he said, lifting the garment up to the light. "What is this technique?"

"*Sashiko*, it means 'little stabs.'" I touched a finger to the heavy stitching.

Developed during the Edo period, *sashiko* had been used for centuries to make fabrics stronger and warmer to combat the brutal winters.

"My *obaasan* taught me the art of *sashiko*. She used to sit me on her lap and let me play with replicating her work in the offcuts as she explained the differences in each pattern."

"The patterns are important?"

I nodded. "The reason we use geometric patterns is because they're evenly distributed." I tugged at the jacket in his hands, demonstrating the lack of give. "It reinforces the material, making the fabric stronger."

"It's rather striking."

A little fusion of annoyance bubbled up in me as I tried to explain its purpose. "It can be beautiful, yes. But more importantly, it's functional. The needle is going through the fabric and leaving the thread behind as a way to strengthen it, protecting the wearer."

Erike hummed under his breath. "And you hand stitched this?"

I nodded.

"It's a good piece. But there is a sadness to your work." He placed the jacket back on the table, raising his eyebrows. "You miss your partner."

I sighed, crossing my arms and leaning a hip against the workbench. "Is it that obvious?"

His lips pursed. "You have the opportunity to be great, Mai. You could fly around the world, host shows in all the major cities. I can see your potential." He tutted. "But you are letting your heart lead you down a road which would jeopardize all this." He shook his head. "What a tragedy that would be."

He tapped his knuckles against the bench then moved on to the next table, examining another of his apprentices.

I bit my lip, not sure how to respond. Erike wanted the best for me—for my designs to be seen by millions, for my pieces to be featured in magazines, for my name to become one which people recognized.

These were dreams that all designers had. And yet, my designs had begun to reflect the hollow ache that had carved its way inside me.

I missed Theo. I missed his smile, his laugh, the way he made me feel like anything was possible when we worked together.

But I had to admit that this separation had also been good for me. It had forced me to reevaluate our relationship —and my dependence on him.

I missed Theo, but each day I survived, I began to realize that I didn't *need* him. I didn't *need* anyone. Sure, it was nice to have them around, and as much as going through panic attacks and living with a horrid anxiety devil sucked, there was power in knowing I could deal with these emotions myself. I didn't need someone to hold my hand constantly. I could hold my own damn hand—and damn if I wasn't proud of myself for that.

I stared down at the designs on the table before me, my mind a whirl of conflicting emotions. Erike was right; this opportunity was everything I had ever dreamt of—to train under his expert guidance, to have my designs recognized and celebrated worldwide—and yet, a crucial piece of *me* was missing.

I ran my fingers over the intricate stitching and elegant lines, thinking of how much better the designs would be if Theo was here helping me. His creative vision, his infectious enthusiasm, the way we pushed each other to be our very best.

I didn't want fame. I wanted Theo.

My phone buzzed and I glanced down, my heart leaping into my throat as I saw my girl's group chat was frantically pushing notifications.

Frowning, I opened the messages.

ANNIE

Mai, I don't want to alarm you, but someone leaked about you and Theo to the press. It's bad. Like, really bad

FRANKIE

They're ripping him apart in the media and your show hasn't even aired. NO ONE EVEN KNOWS HIM!

FLO

What's happened?

ANNIE

Someone leaked that Mai and Theo were faking their relationship. They're saying she should have her prize withdrawn

FLO

Who would even know about her winning?

ANNIE

I don't know, but I'm about to fucking
find out

FRANKIE

Annie, calm down

ANNIE

I will fucking not. This is my favorite
brother-in-law, and one of my best friends.
You better bet your ass I'm throwing down
for them

FLO

You only have one brother-in-law

ANNIE

Beside the point

FLO

Mai? You there? Do you need us to fly to
Italy?

FRANKIE

I'm googling flights

ANNIE

I'm calling a Linc. Let me know when the
flights are booked

I closed the chat and navigated to a news app, scanning the damaging article.

"Oh God."

It laid it all out. There were times and dates, examples of Theo's past "transgressions." They painted him as a cheater, and me as a naive little girl at best, and a cunning fraudster at worst.

The worst part was, they weren't too far off the truth for that second one.

How could this have happened? Theo and I had been

so careful to keep up our façade. Everyone had believed we were the real deal. And now it was all crashing down around us.

Erike cleared his throat, drawing my attention. "Is everything alright, Mai?" His brow furrowed with concern as he and the other intern stared at me.

I swallowed hard, debating how much to tell him. "It's... there's some bad press. About me and Theo. Someone is saying our relationship was fake, that we deceived everyone."

Erike's eyes widened slightly. "I see."

Did he? Cause I didn't.

He gestured at my phone. "Perhaps you should call him. No doubt the network will be in touch shortly."

"Of course." I stepped away from my table. "Excuse me."

Power walking out into the late afternoon sunlight, I took a deep breath of the warm air, trying to find my center.

I found a quiet spot in a nearby courtyard and, with shaking hands, dialed Theo's number. It rang once, twice, three times before he finally picked up.

"Mai." He sounded exhausted.

"Theo, have you seen the news? How did this happen?"

"Fuck, Mai. I'm sorry." He sighed heavily. "I'm pretty sure it was Jude. He confronted me in the bathroom during the finale and threatened to expose us. I guess he made good on that threat."

My blood ran cold.

"What are you talking about?"

Theo didn't answer.

I pulled the phone away from my ear, checking the connection. "Hello?"

"I'm here. I just…. He tried to blackmail me into throwing the competition."

"He did *what*?" I began to pace, trying to comprehend the shit show Theo had just admitted to. "How?"

"He said he'd leak those texts. That he knew people who could ruin us. Ruin you."

"Why didn't you tell me? Is that why you were so off in the final round? Wait." I stilled. "Were you going to do it?"

"Yeah," Theo admitted.

"Why?"

"I wanted to protect you. The idea of you being hurt—of you being exposed to hate—it makes me fucking livid."

I could hear the rage simmering in his tone.

I stared off into the distance, my gaze unfocussed. "But then you pulled it together and helped me. Why?"

"Watching you in action, seeing how passionately dedicated you are, how fucking hard you work, how hard you were fighting despite your fear—you deserved to win." He cleared his throat. "There was no way I was going to destroy your chance at the prize."

I shook my head, trying to clear it. "You never said anything."

"I was going to tell you later that night but we…." he trailed off meaningfully.

A blush touched my cheeks. "We distracted each other."

"That's one way to put it." He swore softly. "I'm sorry, Mai. When we didn't win and then I didn't hear anything from Jude, I assumed he'd leave it alone. I should have told you."

"Yeah, you should have."

We were quiet for a beat.

"What are we going to do?" I asked, hearing the tremble in my voice. "The network, the media, everyone will be demanding answers."

"I don't know. Deny it? We're a couple, right? Does it really matter about timing?"

"We are but...." I bit my lip, mind racing. "Theo, I don't want to lie anymore."

"What are you saying?" His tone sounded guarded.

I took a deep breath. "I'm saying, I think we need to come clean. Admit the truth and let the network decide what they want to do."

Relief made my knees weak, and I took two steps across the small courtyard to sink onto an old bench.

"But your prize, your reputation—Mai, this could ruin everything you've worked for."

My resolved strengthened. "We need to do what's right."

"Give me twenty-four hours, please. Let me fix this."

I brushed hair away from my face and tilted my head back, staring up at the autumn sun.

"How?"

"Trust me. Please."

"Twenty-four hours," I agreed reluctantly. "But, Theo, if this gets any worse—"

"It won't," he promised. "I'll handle it. Just focus on your internship and leave the rest to me."

We said our goodbyes and I hung up, staring at my

phone screen. The unanswered texts and notifications seemed to mock me. How had everything unraveled so quickly?

"Because you lied." I closed my eyes, pinching the bridge of my nose.

Theo and I may have gotten together, but we'd started out as a lie, and I couldn't deny that fact. I needed to own it.

But first, I needed to trust him.

Sighing, I squared my shoulders and marched back into the studio, determined to throw myself into my work.

Erike glanced up. "Are you done with your personal issue?"

I nodded.

"Good." Erike gestured at my table. "Shall we get back to it then? I have some thoughts on your color story."

Grateful for the distraction, I lost myself in the work, trying to ignore the niggle in my heart that said Theo needed me.

CHAPTER 19
THEO

There's no good way to admit you've lied. My foot jiggled on the cool concrete floor as Celeste stared me down over her desk.

Around us, light techs, sound engineers, and people whose job I had no clue about ran here and there, avoiding their boss like the plague.

"You're sorry," she said finally, her tone icy. "Forgive me if I find that hard to believe."

I winced. "If it makes you feel better, karma has certainly bitten me on the ass."

"It does," she said, absently stirring a pencil in her

coffee. I opened my mouth to say something when one of her assistants caught my eye, frantically shaking his head.

I snapped my mouth shut.

"Do you know who sold you out?"

"Jude." I leaned back in my chair. "Though I'm not sure why when they won the competition."

"Interesting." Celeste tapped her pencil against the mug. "You know, you film well. It's a shame you're in such a pickle."

"I know how bad this looks," I said, leaning forward in my chair. "But you have to believe me when I say that we never meant for it to go this far. It got out of hand."

She scoffed. "Out of hand? Theo, you and Mai straight up lied. To me, to the network, to the viewers. This isn't some minor transgression. You perpetuated your lie for the entirety of filming. Do you have any idea the damage control I'm going to have to do? The network is already breathing down my neck demanding answers."

I ran a hand through my hair. "I'll do whatever it takes to make this right. Interviews, press releases, public apologies—you name it."

"And what about Mai? Is she on board with this little plan of yours?" Celeste asked pointedly.

I hesitated. "Mai wants to come clean, admit everything."

Celeste leaned back in her chair, studying me intently. "And you? What do you want?"

I met her steely gaze. "I want to protect her. She doesn't deserve to have her reputation ruined over this. Let me take the fall."

She raised an eyebrow. "How noble of you. But how exactly do you plan to 'take the fall', as you put it?"

I took a deep breath. "I'll release a statement saying the fake relationship was my idea. That I coerced Mai into going along with it for publicity. She's innocent in all this."

"You really think anyone will believe that? You two looked pretty cozy together by the end there." Her tone was skeptical.

I shrugged helplessly. "It's the truth, mostly. Mai never wanted to do this. I convinced her we should."

Celeste sighed heavily, tapping her manicured nails on the desk. "You better hope she corroborates your story. If there's even a hint that this 'relationship' took advantage of her in any way...." She let the threat hang.

"I understand."

She took a sip of her coffee, watching me over the rim.

"You're pretty gone for this girl, aren't you?"

The words I wanted to say to Mai burned on my tongue.

I love you.

"She's a good woman."

Celeste snorted. "I'm a good woman, that girl is a fucking saint. Do you have any idea how many people we have come through these doors looking to be TV stars?"

She paused and I shook my head, realizing belatedly that she expected an answer.

"Thousands each week. And from those thousands at the last fucking minute, we pull you two. It's the perfect pairing. A funny small-town boy and his girlfriend with big dreams. You two should be the darlings of the screen, a director's delight. You've turned into my fucking nightmare."

She placed her coffee on the desk. "Here's what we're gonna do. I'm gonna fix this for you. But you have to do something for me."

"Anything."

She chuckled darkly. "Oh, honey. You have no idea what you just agreed to."

I ignored her ominous words. "What do you need me to do?"

Celeste smiled, a slow, calculating curl of her lips. "You, Theo, are going to give the performance of a lifetime. We're going to spin this little 'fake relationship' revelation in our favor."

"How so?"

She leaned forward, steepling her fingers. "Picture this —a heartfelt confession on live TV. You admit that yes, initially you and Mai agreed to pretend to be a couple for the show. But somewhere along the way, real feelings developed. By the end, you were both head over heels, your on-screen chemistry impossible to fake."

"You really think anyone is gonna believe us after this?"

Celeste chuckled. "I love when a TV land newbie joins the crew. You're always so naive. Our viewers will eat this shit up. Star-crossed lovers who found each other under unconventional circumstances? It's reality TV gold."

I shook my head. "Mai will never agree to this. She wants to come clean, be done with the lies, not create more."

"Is it really a lie though?"

I rocked back in my seat. *Jesus Christ. How did she—*

"I know all, Theo. Does she feel the same way about you?"

I lifted one shoulder. "You'd have to ask her."

"Good answer." Celeste leaned back in her seat. "Alternatively, there is another option."

I hated to ask. "And that is?"

"It's time for your solo, Mr. Garrett."

CHAPTER 20
MAI

MAI

I miss you

THEO

Ditto times infinity

MAI

That's a lot of missing

THEO

T-minus 24 hours and counting….

I'd spent my final week of the internship working around the clock to deliver on the pieces Erike wanted me to display—ones he'd be proud to endorse. Our show started in less than three hours.

I paced nervously in the quiet backstage area, my heels clicking on the polished floor.

Just a few weeks ago, I'd been a small-town girl with big fashion dreams. And now, thanks to Erike's mentorship and this incredible opportunity, those dreams were within reach. But I couldn't fully savor the moment, not with the weight of our deception hanging over me.

I pulled out my phone to check my messages and winced. My inbox continued to explode with abusive messages from strangers. The show hadn't even aired yet, and already they'd made assumptions about me and Theo.

I hit delete all and tucked the phone back in my pocket as I attempted to calm my nerves.

"Hey, you okay?"

I turned to find Frankie, Flo and Annie walking my way.

"How was the museum?" I asked, forcing a smile.

My best friends had dropped everything to fly out here and support me. The last week had involved copious amounts of gelato, lots of tears, and far too much red wine.

"I got to touch David's dick," Flo enthused, holding up her fingers and wiggling them.

"The museum had a special accessible wing," Frankie explained. "Which included a touchable replica of Michelangelo's David."

"He seemed cold," Flo said, using her cane to search for a seat. "Or shy."

I snorted. "The man has had his junk stared at by billions of people. I don't think he's shy."

"How you doing?" Annie asked, wrapping an arm around my shoulders. "You ready for tonight?"

I swallowed, glancing at the multitudes of empty chairs around the warehouse. "I'm trying not to think about it."

Annie slung an arm around my shoulders. "You'll do great. You've worked hard for this."

"I'm worried that someone might derail it. The public backlash has been brutal."

My fingers began to dance across my thumb, tapping out a familiar beat.

Flo propped her chin on her hand. "I know it's hard to ignore their negativity, but don't give them your peace. They don't know you or Theo."

"Speaking of...." Frankie spun her chair until she was seated beside Flo and adopted the same pose. "Tell us more about you and the delectable Mr. Garrett."

"Yes," Annie agreed, taking the seat on Flo's other side, also propping her chin on her hand as she looked at me with a cheeky grin. "All the glory details please."

"I believe the saying is 'gory details,'" I said, crossing my arms.

"Not if it involves multiple orgasms."

Snorting, I too took a seat, opting to sit facing them. "It's complicated."

"He's a man. They overcomplicate everything," Annie said with a very expressive wave of her hand.

"He believes in me." I shook my head with a laugh. "And he's proud of me? As in genuinely delighted by my achievements. It's...."

"Wonderful," Flo breathed with a happy little sigh. "He cares for you."

"He's also...." I blushed.

Frankie leaned forward. "Ah, now we get to the bedroom. I recognize that look. Spill, missy."

"He's respectfully aggressive. Like he'll throw me around the bedroom but he'll check to see if I want that first."

"Consent," Frankie said with an approving nod. "Good man."

"I wish someone would throw me around a bedroom," Flo muttered, her bottom lip jutting out. "All anyone does is compliment me on my ability to walk from one side of a room to another without tripping."

Annie patted her leg. "You'll find your person."

"They better hurry up. My patience is wearing thin."

"Back to Mai," Frankie encouraged, gesturing for me to continue.

"I know it's quick—"

"It's not," Flo interrupted. "You've been dating for years —you just didn't know it."

"But a friendship relationship is different to a romantic relationship," Frankie pointed out reasonably. "And moving from one to the other requires courage and open communication. It also requires you to grapple with the reality that it might not work—and to move through that pain."

I nodded. "That's part of it. I'm worried that this won't work out and I'll lose him. He makes my life better in so many significant and simple ways."

"You want to explore this with him but you're worried it will break what you have."

I blew out a breath at Flo's statement. "Yeah."

Flo tilted her head to one side. "Do you trust him?"

"Yes."

"Then trust he'll have a care with your heart."

Flo's words cut through my doubts. I trusted Theo. He'd supported me through this wild adventure—and had laid his own feelings on the line. I needed to trust that whatever happened, we'd navigate our way through it.

"Ouch!" Annie clutched at her chest. "Damn, girl. Way to lay that truth down."

"I'm not going to lie." Frankie grinned. "You and Theo? I didn't pick it."

"Odd bunch," Annie agreed. She flicked her thumb in Flo's direction. "Always assumed he'd end up with this one."

"She's pointing at you, Flo," I said, rolling my eyes.

"Theo and me?" Flo made a face. "God no. Could you imagine? We're both too optimistic. We need someone to be the realist in the relationship."

Annie rose from her seat and walked across to place her hands on my shoulders, staring into my eyes.

"What you and Theo have is worth fighting for. I'm going to channel my inner Flo right now and say something super mushy."

"I can't wait to hear this," Flo muttered to Frankie.

"You and Theo make sense. You challenge him in ways no one else can. He's been clocking in on life for a long time. Being with you is good for him."

"And for you," Frankie agreed, pushing her chair forward until her wheels brushed the side of my seat. "He's helped you find your confidence."

I blinked rapidly, fighting tears that threatened to fall. "I love you guys."

"Nawww." Flo rose up, reaching out a hand for Annie to help guide her across to me. "Group hug!"

We leaned down until we could wrap Frankie in our four-way hug, squeezing tight.

"Alright," Annie said after a beat, breaking up our love fest. "We need to head back to the hotel and get ready for tonight. You okay if we leave you?"

I nodded. "I'll be fine."

"When does your family fly in?" Flo asked, digging through her bag.

I glanced at my watch. "Their plane should have arrived by now. Ren said they'd catch up with me after the event."

"We'll try and meet them at the hotel."

I waved them off, watching them leave the venue.

Slowly, I walked around the backstage area, keeping myself busy as I twisted the ring on my middle finger. Nerves began to build as I contemplated tonight's show.

Everything will be fine. You've worked hard, the models are great, your designs are Erike approved. Everything will be fine.

"Mai?"

I turned to see one of the network's camera guys waving at me. "Can we get you out front please?"

I followed him around to the front of house where my models were being positioned on stage for different shots.

In all, there were twenty-six designs, each incredibly unique and gorgeous. My chest ached seeing them, knowing I had done that. I had created these exceptional pieces.

"You mind if we get some shots of you?" the camera guy asked, gesturing toward the stage. "Be cool to be able to slice you in on these."

I nodded, forcing a smile. "Of course."

We took shots, and they were about to finish when I heard a familiar foot fall.

Theo.

I turned, seeing him standing at the end of the runway, the corner of his mouth lifted into a wry grin. His hair needed a cut, and stubble decorated his cheeks, and he wore a tailored suit that fit so nicely my heart flipped at the sight of him.

"Hey, Ms. Winner," he greeted, opening his arms wide. "Can I get a hug?"

A sob choked me, and I stumbled forward, tumbling down the runway toward him. He caught me easily, hugging me close.

He cupped my cheeks, pressing kisses over my cheeks, holding me close as I fought for control.

"Theo."

"Missed you," he murmured against my lips. "So fucking much."

Our kiss was fierce and desperate, our hands grasping at each other as if we were alone and naked.

"Phew," someone said from behind me. "You better be getting this on camera, Phil."

"Every second," Phil confirmed.

I pulled back from Theo, suddenly remembering we were far from alone. He murmured a protest but let me go.

"I can't believe you're here," I whispered, searching his face. "How?"

Theo's expression remained calm and reassuring. "I'm here to support you, Mai. I wouldn't miss this for the world."

I swallowed. "But what about—"

"It's taken care of."

I frowned. "Theo, I don't want any more lies or—"

"Hey," he hushed me gently, brushing a thumb over my lips. "Do you trust me?"

I gazed into his eyes, seeing the earnestness there, and I nodded. "Yes."

"Relax," Theo said with a small smile. "Everything is going to be fine. I promise."

Before I could question him further, a production assistant appeared, headset on. "Two minutes to showtime, lovebirds! Places please."

"Places?" I asked, confused as fuck. My show wasn't due to start for another hour.

Theo caught my hand and pulled me toward the middle of the stage—where two men had carried a couch, positioning it just so.

"Don't worry. We're just going to do another interview with Michelle. No biggie," Theo said, trying to reassure me.

I took a deep breath, trying to center myself and work out what the fuck was happening.

Theo helped me sit, then did the same as a camera crew quickly set up a small tripod. A moment later, Michelle appeared, smiling large.

"Hey, you two," she said, taking a seat. "I hear today is going to be a great day!"

A guy with a clapboard came up, holding it near my head.

"And in three, two, one. Action!"

He stepped back, and I tried to act normal as Michelle introduced the viewers to *Perfect Fit*.

Am I in the twilight zone? Haven't we already done this?

"Now, Theo," Michelle said with an easy grin. "Tell me, how long have you and Mai been dating?"

"Officially?" He glanced over at me. "She still hasn't said yes. Unofficially? Years."

She leaned forward in her seat. "That's interesting. Our sources have indicated that you might have a few recent dating skeletons in the closet."

Theo chuckled, placing a hand over mine, halting my nervous twisting of my ring by offering me the reassuring I needed.

"I kept dating after meeting Mai because she didn't seem interested. I assumed I'd meet someone but I never did."

"Why not?"

"Because it's always been her."

My breath caught. He squeezed my hand, his gaze warm, his lips curving up at the sides.

"I tried, you know. But every time I went on a date, I kept wanting to be with you. Tell you the joke I was about to crack, or the story I was about to tell. I wanted to order extra fries and share a plate of chicken wings. Or walk down the street reminiscing about silly shit from our childhoods."

He lifted my hand to his mouth, brushing a kiss against my knuckles. "You're it for me, Mai. You always have been. It might have taken lying about the seriousness of our relationship to bring us together, but we were never fake. You've had my heart for years. And I just need you to know that."

My heart pounded in my chest. I wanted so badly to believe this was real—that his words were genuine and not for the cameras.

"Is this real?" I asked softly, searching his face. "Or is this just another lie?"

He brushed the hair from my cheek. "Real. The way I feel about you is real. I love you, Mai. I want to have a future with you."

I searched his face, seeing nothing but truth written there.

Any fears I had dissipated. We were shifting into new territory that at once felt scary and so utterly right—and I trusted him to hold my heart.

I melted, sinking against him. "I love you too."

The cameras and crew faded away, until it was just us and this perfect moment.

"I mean it," he said softly. "You're my one. The end game."

I huffed out a laugh. "Then kiss me like you mean it."

He chuckled. "Yes, ma'am."

Theo captured my lips in a deep, soulful kiss that seared away the longing, the confusion, the yearning. My doubts vanished as our mouths moved together. His strong hands cupped my face tenderly as he angled his head to deepen the kiss. My fingers slid into his thick hair, holding him close, never wanting this perfection to end.

Someone nearby cleared their throat. "Uh, guys? The cameras are still rolling."

We broke apart, breathless and flushed. Michelle looked on with an amused grin.

"Well, I think that passionate display just removed any lingering doubts about the authenticity of your relationship!" She chuckled. "Why don't we take a quick break and then we'll resume."

Theo hauled me up, leading me through the backstage area to a private dressing room. Once inside, I turned to face Theo, my pulse racing.

"What you said... did you mean it?"

Theo's expression was open and sincere as he took both my hands in his. "Every word, Mai. I never should have let things get this far without being honest about my feelings for you. I love you."

Tears pricked my eyes. "I've been in love with you for so long. I just never thought you saw me as more than a friend."

He gasped playfully. "Shame on you for not giving in to my animal magnetism." He cupped my face tenderly. "You're my everything, Mai. My partner, my best friend, the love of my life. I don't want to spend another day without you knowing that."

A giddy laugh bubbled up from my chest. "I love you so much."

"So we're official?" he asked, kissing his way down my neck.

I tilted my head back, giving him better access. "Let's not be too hasty."

"I'll show you hasty."

Our lips met again, soft and sweet this time, sealing our declarations with a promise. When we finally parted, I rested my forehead against his.

"What do we do now?" I asked.

"Anal?"

"Theo!"

He chuckled. "Nothing, babe. The footage is just for us. Michelle agreed because I didn't know how else to tell you.

Celeste—who likes me, I told you she'd come around—spoke to the producers. They've agreed to let us re-film and to edit parts of the program before it goes to air. We'll be able to tell our real story."

"Really?"

"Mm." He winced. "On one condition."

"And that is?"

He cleared his throat. "She told me about your pitch for *Theo Tries*."

I stiffened. "Are you okay with that? I wanted to tell you, but I didn't want to get your hopes up and—"

His lips curved into a wry smile. "Okay? Mai, you're a fucking genius. I haven't been this excited since—" His gaze dropped to my breasts. "Well, you know."

I snorted, shoving him. "Tell me more. When does filming start? Where is Celeste sending you first? Are you nervous? Where do you want to go?"

"Later." He kissed my forehead, then my cheek, working his way down to my neck. "We have something more important to do."

"And *that* is?" I repeated, tilting my head to give him greater access.

"Make love in this room."

I laughed, then groaned as Theo's lips found that sensitive spot behind my ear.

His deep voice rumbled against my skin. "I need you, Mai. I want to worship every inch of your gorgeous body. Let me show you exactly how much I adore you."

A shiver of anticipation raced down my spine. "What are you waiting for?"

Theo's answering grin was positively wicked. In a flash,

he scooped me up and carried me over to the plush sofa, laying me down gently. He hovered over me, his eyes dark with desire.

"You're so beautiful," he murmured reverently. "I can't believe I get to call you mine."

My heart swooned. I reached up to caress his jaw, the stubble rasping against my fingers. "I've always been yours, Theo. Now and forever."

Our mouths crashed together in a heated kiss, lips and tongues tangling. Theo's strong hands roamed my body, setting my skin ablaze. I arched into his touch, desperate to be closer, needing him.

We made quick work of our clothes, our movements frantic. When there was finally nothing between us but skin, Theo paused, his gaze drinking me in as he rolled on a condom.

"Perfection," he breathed. "Absolute perfection."

"I could say the same."

We came together in a crash of limbs and breaths. Driving each other higher with teasing and taunts, our bodies moved together in perfect unity.

"I love you," I cried, coming around his thick cock.

"Fuck, I love you too," he groaned, and I relished the desperation in his declaration.

We lay together, snuggling on the couch in the aftermath.

"Happy?"

I traced a pattern across his chest, reflecting. I'd achieved more than I'd ever dreamed, and I felt lucky to have experienced it with my best friend by my side.

My answer was a non-issue.

"Blissfully so," I admitted, pressing a kiss to his chest. "You?"

"Of course." He pulled me closer. "I've got my whole world right here."

"Oh, that's slick." I giggled, letting him kiss my ear.

Our moment of peace was spectacularly shattered when I heard the doorknob turn.

"Mai?" Ren called. "You in here?"

Theo rolled me under him, his bare ass presented toward the door. "Get the fuck out!"

The door's momentum halted.

"Theo?" Ren sounded confused.

"Yes," he ground out, ignoring my hysterical silent giggles. "Can you give us a minute?"

The door remained partially open.

"By us do you mean...?"

Theo mumbled something under his breath then lifted his head. "If you walk through that door, you're getting something knitted for Christmas!"

I stared up at him, baffled by this declaration, but Ren appeared to understand.

"Good to know. We'll see you both shortly." As he pulled the door closed, I heard my mother asking why they couldn't see me.

"They're filming," my brother lied. "Let's go see if there's somewhere we can get some coffee."

Door firmly shut, I fell into body-shaking laughter, gasping for breath as tears ran down my face.

"Oh, laugh it up," Theo muttered, pushing away from the couch with a small smile. "Your grandmother nearly saw my ass."

I slowly sobered, wiping the tears of amusement from my cheeks. "I'm sorry, but it is hilarious."

"Mm." He handed me my clothing, brushing a kiss across my forehead. "Certainly one to tell the grandkids."

My heart flip-flopped a little in my chest at the casual mention of our future.

We dressed and found my family claiming prime seats in front of the runway. My grandparents, parents and siblings had made the journey—on the network's dime—and the cameras caught every minute of our reunion.

"Proud of you," my *obaasan* whispered, tears shimmering on her lashes. "Enjoy tonight."

I farewelled them before heading backstage, my nerves beginning to rise.

I touched the ring on my finger three times before lifting my hand to my mouth and pretending to eat. It didn't help lessen my anxiety, but it did make it more bearable.

Models, staging assistants, production crew, and cameras bustled about and for a while it seemed everyone needed my attention.

"How would you like her hair?"

"Is this fit correct?"

"Do you want a dark eyeshadow or a light to offset the dress?"

"Mai, this jacket seems to be too short in the arms."

"Could you give me a moment?" I'd asked at one point, needing a second to breathe. "I'm feeling a little panicked."

The crew backed off, the models taking the pause to sip their drinks or chat with each other about their other shows.

No one protested or judged me. No one even cared that I was enforcing a boundary. They just did it.

It was only as I took my place in the wings of the stage as the lights dimmed and the music slowly rose that I realized what I'd done.

I'd survived.

No.

I'd *thrived*. I'd been anxious, fretting, nervous. I'd experienced a rollercoaster of emotions today, and yet I'd pushed through it.

I peeked out of the wings, searching the crowd. There, front and center, sat my beautiful family and friends.

"Are you ready?"

I turned to find Erike standing behind me looking rather dashing in a three-piece suit.

"No," I answered with a small grin. "But let's do it anyway."

He linked arms with me, standing beside me as he nodded to the stage manager who began the official countdown.

"You should be proud of yourself. You've done an excellent job."

"I am," I agreed, surprised to find that I wasn't lying.

"Good." He squeezed my arm. "Now enjoy *your* show."

The music blared as the first model stepped out onto the stage, the light catching on the red and pink pattern of her dress.

I heard the sound of approval from the audience, and breathed out a long sigh of relief.

The music continued as each model strode confidently down the catwalk, showing off the designs I'd poured my soul into.

With a flourish, the music finished and Erike gave me a little push toward the stage.

"Your turn," he murmured as I stepped out, my heart in my throat.

The crowd rose to their feet, applause thundering down toward me as the models parted and I stepped into the spotlight.

I raised a hand, giving a little wave of acknowledgement as the applause continued.

I narrowed my gaze, finding my family as they celebrated my moment.

Frankie, Jay, Annie and Linc were on one side, clapping and cheering. Next were my parents, beaming with pride. My grandparents were still seated, but both smiling widely as they clapped, stomping their feet. Beside them stood my sister and her partner. Keiko held up an iPad, turning it around for me to see Yasmin and Maeve waving frantically on the screen.

I laughed, waving back.

Finally, Ren stood with his arm around Flo as he whispered in her ear. She waved, and I blew them a kiss, grinning when Ren whispered once again in her ear—no doubt telling her I'd seen her.

But it was the man in the dashing suit jacket that caught my attention.

Theo's smile beamed at me, the pride shining in his eyes. Our gazes caught.

"I love you," he mouthed at me, his words swept away by the crowd. "Proud of you."

Tears clogged the back of my throat as I took a breath

and glanced around, committing every second of this moment to memory.

Staring back at him, I smiled.

EPILOGUE
MAI

Theo flopped onto the couch beside me, plopping a large bowl of popcorn in my lap.

"Yasmin," I said into my phone, grinning up at him. "It's fine. Maeve and I are co-owners for a reason, right? Let us handle it and you focus on little Charlie, okay?"

She breathed heavily down the phone line. "I'm sorry. I'm just...."

"Exhausted, stressed, sick?"

She chuckled. "Something like that."

"Seriously," I reassured her. "We're good. Take the rest of the week off and we'll see you when you're better."

"Thanks, Mai. Love you."

"Love you too. Later."

I hung up and tossed the phone onto the coffee table, digging my hand into the popcorn as I shifted to snuggle into his side on our couch.

"Everything okay?" he asked, wrapping an arm around my shoulder.

"Charlie's sick. Yasmin's freaking out."

"Babies get sick," Theo said with an air of experience I didn't feel he had.

I chuckled, tipping my head back to look at him. "You okay if I pull a few extra hours at the store this week?"

"At *your* store," he corrected, leaning down to kiss me. "And of course. Live your dream, babe."

I sighed happily, snuggling closer as he hit play on the remote.

"What's this episode about?" I asked as the opening credits scrolled across the screen.

"I can't remember."

I glanced up, cocking an eyebrow. "You can't remember?"

He shook his head. "Guess we'll both be surprised."

I snorted, turning back to watch the show.

"Welcome to *Theo Tries*, the show where I travel the country trying different jobs."

The video cut to Theo standing outside a fancy-looking wedding venue, a huge smile on his face.

"I've always wondered what it takes to pull off the perfect wedding," TV Theo said. "Today I'm going to find out by shadowing renowned wedding planner Alicia Hsu."

The camera panned to an elegant woman who shook Theo's hand. "Ready to dive in to the wonderful world of weddings?" Alicia asked with a grin.

"Absolutely! I'm yours to command," Theo replied cheerfully.

I couldn't help but laugh at Theo's signature enthusiasm and eagerness to learn.

I'd forever be grateful to Celeste for helping make this happen. Not only had she helped us reedit our cuts to present a truthful reflection of our time—and relationship status—on *Perfect Fit*, but she'd personally championed Theo's career. With the wave of her magic clipboard, she'd smoothed everything over, paving the way for Theo's career.

It further helped that Jude and Keeley got their comeuppance thanks to a fraud enquiry. They'd needed the money from both the contest and selling us out in order to try and cover their tracks. Turned out, they'd fudged their business accounts—committing wire and tax fraud.

Unfortunately for them, the authorities had worked out their scheme before the prize money could be handed over. Last I'd heard, they were awaiting trial.

When news of their arrest had broken, any attention that had remained pointed at Theo and I had dissipated, leaving us free to get on with our lives.

On screen, Alicia began showing Theo around the

venue, pointing out the ceremony and reception spaces and explaining the timeline for the day.

"The key is organization and staying on top of all the little details," Alicia said. "A great wedding coordinator has to be unflappable under pressure."

Theo nodded intently. The cameras then followed him as he helped set up centerpieces, lined up the wedding party for the processional, and dealt with a near-disaster with the cake delivery. Through it all, TV Theo maintained his upbeat attitude and quick wit.

Beside me, the real Theo chuckled. "I'm surprised they didn't show me—"

TV Theo tripped, nearly toppling a tower of champagne flutes in the process.

"—never mind."

Now laughing, I snuggled closer to my boyfriend, enjoying our easy companionship.

Our lives were busy, so nights like tonight were precious. Between Theo's wildly popular show, and my never-ending custom orders, I could safely say we'd managed to become successes.

The credits rolled and I tilted my head back, smiling up at him. "What's next on the list of things for Theo to try?"

He hesitated, then lifted, shuffling me around until he could reach between the couch cushions.

I watched, my heart in my mouth when he withdrew a small black box.

"I thought we might do a special episode," he said, his voice gruff with emotion. "Theo tries marriage."

I cleared my throat, blinking rapidly to keep the tears at bay. "What's special about it?"

"It airs twenty-four hours a day, seven days a week just for you."

A hysterical bubble of laughter caught in my throat.

"Mai Sakamoto, will you do me the honor of—"

"Yes!" I threw myself at him. "Yes, yes, yes!"

"Oof!" Theo laughed, wrapping me in a hug. "You don't know what I was going to say!"

"It's always a yes," I told him, peppering his face with kisses.

Theo tenderly cupped my face, his green eyes dancing.

"I can't wait to spend the rest of my life with you," he murmured, brushing his thumb over my cheekbone.

Tears pricked my eyes. "It's going to be an adventure."

He chuckled. "That's the best kind of life." He kissed me softly, reverently, like I was the most precious thing in his world.

"I love you," I whispered against his lips. "Even if it's too late to win your bet with Ren. We could have really used that hundred bucks for the wedding."

He barked out a laugh. "Damn bet." Rolling me over, he covered me with his body.

"I love you," he whispered, sealing his words with a kiss.

Theo slid the ring on my finger, and like our relationship, it was a perfect fit.

Thank you for reading Darn Knit All.
I hope you fell in love with Theo and Mai, and
their gorgeous love story.

Want more Evie Mitchell books? Check out my website at

EvieMitchell.com

If you enter the code **EBOOK10** you can get 10% off your purchase from my website.

Be sure to also sign up for my newsletter for more discounts, sneak peeks, and bookish news.

TRANSLATIONS

Kimono (着物) - Japanese traditional clothing (esp. full-length). Traditionally a wrapped-front garment with square sleeves and a rectangular body, and is worn left side wrapped over right, unless the wearer is deceased

Seiza (正座) – kneeling

Hitowonomu (人を飲む) – to write the kanji for "person" on one's hand three times and mimic swallowing them as a technique for calming one's nerves

Hito (人) – person

Kanji (漢字) – the logographic Chinese characters adapted from the Chinese script used in the writing of Japanese

Haha (母 / はは) – mother, used when talking about your own mother to other people

Temiyage (手土産) – thank-you gifts, commonly given when you're visiting someone's home as a sign of thanks

Obaasan (おばあさん) – grandmother, used when referring to someone else's grandmother or addressing your own in her presence

Ojiisan (お爺さん) – grandfather, used when speaking about your grandfather or someone else's grandfather

Mizu ni nagasu (水に流す) – which means "the water flows", and is the equivalent of the English saying "water under the bridge" or "forgive and forget'"

Origami (折り紙) – from ori meaning "folding" and kami meaning "paper", is the Japanese art of paper folding

Sashiko (刺し子) – "little stabs", a type of traditional Japanese embroidery or stitching used for the decorative and/or functional reinforcement of cloth and clothing

AUTHOR NOTE AND ACKNOWLEDGEMENTS

Dear Gorgeous Reader,

I would like to take a moment to thank the many people who supported this book.

To you, my dearest greedy reader, goes a special thanks. Thank you to everyone who asked for Mai and Theo's book, and who waited impatiently for it. Thank you to those who read this series and loved it, shared it, and told me about it. When I tell people that our greedy reader group is the best, most supportive community out there, I tell no lies!

Thank you to Meena, Kevin, Izumi, and the expert readers who wish to remain anonymous. Your advice, guidance, and support have helped shape Darn Knit All.

Thank you also to the editors and readers from Salt and Sage Books, Emerald Edits, Aquila Editing, and Evermore Editing. Your time and efforts are invaluable.

Thank you to Lyric, and especially Brittney, Natalie, and Liam for helping bring this book to life in audio.

Thank you to Laras and Eileen who illustrated the most perfect covers for this series.

Thank you to Liz, Nina, Jodie, Megan, Lana, and Bec who supported me when I thought I would break, and who celebrated every win. You are truly incredible, and I love and am grateful for each of you.

All credit needs to go to my husband. When I said I

wanted to be a full-time writer, he didn't hesitate. He told me to take a chance at making my dreams come true. Thank you for being the generous, funny, kind, caring, intelligent, witty, and damned sexy man that you are. Thank you for always dancing when I know you hate dancing. Thank you for the air high-fives and butt slaps. The shared laughs, and knowing looks. Thank you for embracing my love of travel and theme parks and puppies (even if you grumble!).

Thank you for our beautiful life together. I love you.

And finally, thank you to me. The past me who struggled through self-doubt and burnout. The me who lives with anxiety and panic attacks. The me who learned how to set boundaries and practice self-care. The me who feels the fear and does it anyway.

Thank you for being brave even when it's hard. Thank you for taking a chance even when it's scary. Thank you for your courage, determination, and self-love.

Darn knit all, we fucking did it.

Sincerely,

Evie Mitchell

Full-time Romance Author

ABOUT THE AUTHOR

Hey, I'm Evie Mitchell.
I'm a thirty-something romance author (she/her/hers) living
with disability. I believe in inclusion, accessibility, and
fierce romance. My loves include steamy romance novels,
my sexy husband, our THREE sausage dogs (THE FUR!!!),
and my ever-growing collection of book-related mugs.

As a woman with a diverse work history, including in areas
such as hospitality, retail, emergency response, event
management, human rights, disability access, and security—
my books are filled with true stories (bridezillas), worst-case
scenarios (malfunctioning zippers), and my favorite tropes
(one-bed).

I'm a strong proponent of #OwnVoices, and specialize in
fiercely inclusive happily ever afters.

EvieMitchell.com
Socials: @EvieMitchellAuthor

ALSO BY EVIE MITCHELL

All Access Series

Knot My Type

Love Flushed

Larsson Siblings

Thunder Thighs

Clean Sweep

The X-List

Reality Check

The Christmas Contract

The A-List

Capricorn Cove

The Shake-up

Double the D

Muffin Top

The Mrs. Clause

New Year, Knew You

Double Breasted

As You Wish

You Sleigh Me

Meat Load

Resolution Revolution

Dogg Pack

Puppy Love

Bad English

The Frock Up

Pier Pressure

Trick or Trent

Reigning Hearts

The Marriage Claim

Silent Knight

Men of Trinity Bay

Kink in the Road

Nameless Souls MC

Runner

Wrath

Ghost

Shield

Elliot Security

Rough Edge

Bleeding Edge